Gentleman Overboard

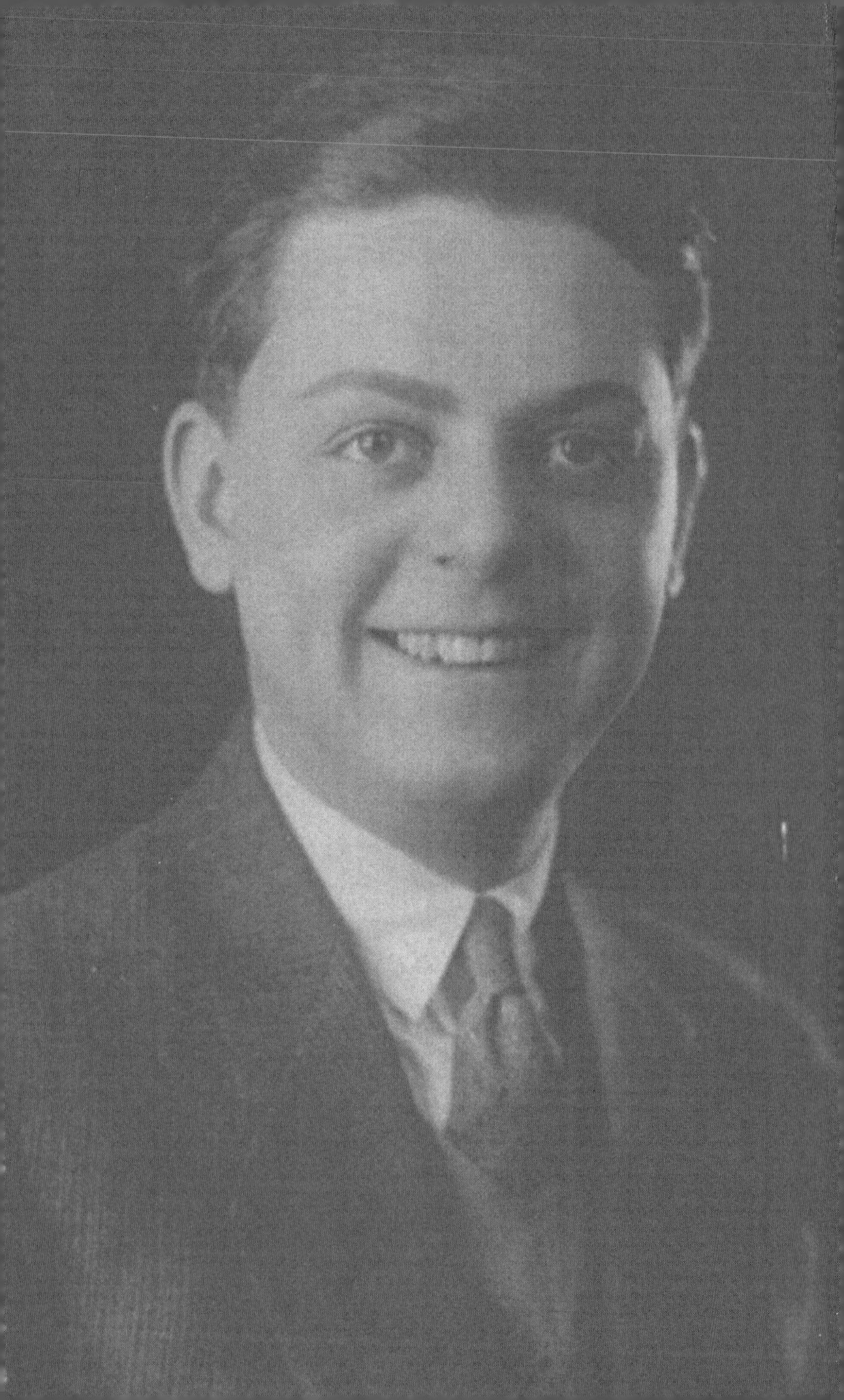

Gentleman Overboard

Herbert Clyde Lewis

Introduction by George Szirtes
Afterword by Brad Bigelow

RECOVERED BOOKS
BOILER HOUSE PRESS

Contents

Introduction

by George Szirtes

The difference between life and death can be no more than a spot of grease. Either it is in the wrong place or you are. One can find oneself at the inside-out edges of life without even trying, like Henry Preston Standish, the central character of Herbert Clyde Lewis's 1937 novel, *Gentleman Overboard*, who slips and falls into the Pacific. Not *man* overboard, you understand, but gentleman, a very proper, decently married-with-children, financially-very-comfortable gentleman.

Being a gentleman does not always help, and it doesn't help Standish who cannot bear to think of himself as any less than the modest, sober, uncomplaining sort of person his background has prepared him to be. If he could bring himself to shout for help somebody might hear him but that would be somewhat embarrassing. Eventually he thinks he should try but no sound comes out of his mouth. Meanwhile the ship is steadily moving away.

There is something inevitable about all of this. Maybe, if your domain is sobriety, you should not risk leaving it. Maybe, if you throw open the door, you should think twice before walking through it. But then what's the point of throwing the door open?

That seems to be the core question of *Gentleman Overboard* but something keeps nagging at us as we wait, and keep waiting, for the boat to turn around and pick up Standish. It is the spectre of existential loneliness, of being, as Coleridge's Ancient Mariner finds.

> Alone, alone, all, all alone
> Alone on a wide, wide sea

Or, as Stevie Smith's drowning figure, in her poem *Not Waving But Drowning* puts it:

> I was much further out than you thought,
> And not waving but drowning.

The others, meanwhile, speculate:

It must have been too cold for him his heart
gave way,
they said

Standish was fine. His heart was sound enough. The other passengers continued with their lives and kept speculating about his absence. But the heart of his author, Herbert Clyde Lewis, did give way, in a lonely room in New York in 1950.

For a book that begins with an accident then simply follows its immediate consequences through to its conclusion, *Gentleman Overboard* is a masterful piece of narrative tension whose chief area of concern is one single consciousness, that of Standish, and it carries the concern through without settling for the easy profundities one might expect given the situation. The consciousness is single but there are other people, it is just that they are elsewhere. Other passengers and crew are seen clearly and briefly. They act, they talk, they think. Their lives goes on: ordinary lives much like Standish's.

Standish is not different: he remains who he is, neither a figure in a melodrama nor a hero in a miraculous adventure. To tell the truth, he is nothing special except in one respect: that on one particular day a vague, niggling discontent – his one authenticating individual choice – had led him to be where he is, on a ship in a rarely frequented part of the Pacific Ocean, his foot on the grease. In other respects his thoughts continue to be essentially banal.

That does not mean the reader is invited to mock him. In fact it is precisely the banality that intrigues us and invites a certain fellow feeling, albeit at a slight distance.

That slight distance is vital. If we over identified with Standish the nature of his predicament would change, as would the ambience of the book. Banality, after all, is not an incidental part of us but a key aspect of our humanity. So we do not see him from the safety of the boat – no one does. We spend most of the time in the sea with him, as if we ourselves were floating in the same wide Pacific, but at a gentlemanly distance. We see him but cannot rescue him.

Lewis's own story echoes Standish's situation. Though he enjoyed some success as a writer and journalist, it was never quite enough to keep him afloat. By the time of his death his star was fading to the point he finally found himself alone in an inner Pacific of his own. There his heart gave way. It must have been too cold for him too.

When we consider the vast number of books and articles published in the English-speaking world in a single month it is a wonder that any survive. Most vanish never to surface again, not necessarily because they are mediocre, but because they have appeared a week too early or late and because the right people did not happen to read them or think to preserve them. The ocean is as deep as the universe for most of us and there are many valuable books and lives lying at the bottom of it. It is a noble project to rescue some of them, to pull them out of the water and say: *Look again! Read this.*

All judgments are interim, as interim as the readers themselves. Standish and Lewis emerge from the depths. For who does not feel adrift on the sea at some point or other, watching the one source of rescue sailing away?

Gentleman Overboard

by Herbert Clyde Lewis

One

When Henry Preston Standish fell headlong into the Pacific Ocean, the sun was just rising on the eastern horizon. The sea was as calm as a lagoon; the weather so balmy and the breeze so gentle that a man could not help but feel gloriously sad. In this part of the Pacific, sunrise was accomplished without fanfare: the sun merely placed her orange dome on the far edge of the great circle and pushed up slowly but persistently until the dim stars had ample time to fade away with the night. In fact, Standish was thinking about the vast difference between the sunrise and the sunset when he took the unfortunate step that landed him in the brine. He was thinking that nature lavished all her generosity on the magnificent sunsets, painting the clouds with streams of colors so brilliant that no man with any sense of beauty could ever forget them. And he was thinking that for some unaccountable reason nature was uncommonly skinflintish with her sunrises over this same ocean.

The S.S. *Arabella* was proceeding methodically from Honolulu to the Canal Zone; in eight more days and nights she would reach Balboa. Few ships traveled the route between Hawaii and Panama; only this one passenger ship every three weeks and an occasional tramp freighter. Foreign vessels seldom had reason to go this way, for the American ships controlled most of the trade with the islands and the bulk of the traffic went to San Pedro, San Francisco, and Seattle. In the thirteen days and nights the *Arabella* had been at sea only one ship had been sighted, going the other way to Hawaii. Standish had not seen it. He had been reading a magazine in his cabin; but the first mate, Mr. Prisk, told him about it later. It was a freighter with some sort of Scandinavian name that he promptly forgot.

The whole trip so far had been so graciously uneventful that Standish never grew tired thanking his lucky star he had decided to sail on the *Arabella.* In a life beset with many cares and duties, as befitted his station, this trip would stand out always as something simple and good. If he never again experienced tranquility he would not fret, for now he knew there was such a thing. His lucky star was the North Star, which was low in the heavens at this latitude, and he had selected it from among all the others because he knew little about stars and it was the easiest to locate and remember.

The *Arabella* was really a freighter with limited passenger accommodations amidships. Eight passengers were aboard besides Standish. There was the remarkably fruitful Mrs. Benson, who had presented her husband with four children in a little more than four and a half years. Mr. Benson himself was not present, but his four images were, three girls and one boy ranging in age from almost zero to three years and eight months. And Mr. Benson might just as well have been along, for Mrs. Benson told Standish all about him. Mr. Benson was a traveling auditor for a bank; somehow they had got separated and now Mrs. Benson was going to join him in Panama.

Of the three remaining passengers, two were missionaries, a Mr. and Mrs. Brown, who seemed to throw up a barrier whenever Standish came near them, as if to suggest that they knew so much more about God than he that there was no use in trying to get friendly. The last of Standish's companions was a Yankee farmer seventy-three years of age, Nat Adams by name, who had no sane explanation for being where he was. After a whole life of honest toil two momentous things had happened all at once: a good crop of potatoes and a severe attack of the wanderlust. He had thrown down the plow and bought travel tickets haphazardly; now aboard the *Arabella* he was Standish's stanch friend, never tiring of expounding the virtues of his set of false teeth, which he pulled out of his mouth and exhibited proudly at the slightest provocation.

The owners of the *Arabella* were not making any money on the trip; there was some talk that the service between Panama and Hawaii would be discontinued next year. Freight was scarce this voyage, and the *Arabella* was partly in ballast. Mr. Prisk was frankly worried, for he was getting on in years and his two children in Baltimore were growing up. He had not seen the children or his wife for three years, but the company automatically sent Mrs. Prisk eighty percent of his salary as first officer, leaving him just about enough to keep him in tobacco and oilskins.

Captain Bell paid no attention to his passengers. He dined with them the first evening out. Then he retired to his cabin and spent the ensuing days in seclusion. Mr. Prisk said the skipper was a fanatic on the subject of ship models, and for the last three voyages had been reproducing a four-masted schooner in miniature. The second and third mates and the engineers and Sparks were all pleasant fellows who had some sort of contract bridge tournament going full blast as soon as one came off watch he would fill in the hand of the man going on. They were nice to the passengers, and Mr. Travis, the chief engineer, showed all who asked the depths of the engine room, but bridge came first. Mr. Prisk, having become first mate through the old-fashioned expedient of starting as an ordinary seaman and working his way up through the ranks, could not play bridge, except the unmentionable auction. Thus he was forced through loneliness to mingle with the passengers once in a while.

From the very start Standish had a wonderful time. Without being unduly mysterious he managed to confine questions pertaining to his own life to a minimum, and spent his time ingeniously prying into the lives of his shipmates. It was not at all hard; all of them (except the missionaries) were more than willing to unburden themselves. Standish observed that he had a powerful urge to discover whatever he could about these people; for the first time in his life he was honestly interested in strange human beings. He would spend hours staring at the wizened face of Nat Adams, or looking into the satisfied blue eyes of Mrs. Benson. And the Benson children were a source of endless delight. Standish admitted to himself he got more pleasure out of little Jimmy and Gladys Benson than he ever had got out of his own two children back in New York, though God knew he loved his own as much as any father. He did not romp with Jimmy and Gladys; he just sat in his comfortable deck chair and watched them do the craziest things. Listening to their hilarious laughter and looking at their healthy bodies and beautifully tanned skins filled Standish with a pleasant kind of melancholy.

The whole trip really was splendid. After the first day out from Honolulu, when the sea was a bit rough, the water became so remarkably smooth that it was like sailing on a glass ocean.

The weather was perfect; that was the only word Standish could find to describe it. In fact, the ordinary superlatives sufficed for Standish in describing the trip to himself. There were things that could not be put into words, such as the colors of the sunsets, the gentle swell of the sea, and the galaxy of stars in the heavens at night. For the rest: the cabin to which he was assigned, the food, the air, the not-too-soft bunk with its clean sheets and sweet-smelling blankets, he thought they were wonderful, marvelous, and magnificent. He ate a lot and took his exercise in the canvas swimming pool rigged up on the well deck, and at night he just sat and smoked his cigarettes and listened to Nat Adams try to explain how the urge to see the world had suddenly assailed a thrifty New England farmer.

He went to bed very early every night, and that explained why he was where he was when he fell into the ocean. Aroused at four o'clock by the tinkle of eight bells on the bridge far forward, Standish lay between the clean sheets for twenty minutes, feeling luxuriously awake. He had turned in at nine o'clock the previous evening, and now it was four-twenty and Standish knew he could not sleep any more. The porthole above his bunk was wide open. He sat up in the bunk and rested his chin on the cold brass. That was a strange sensation, sending delightful shivers down his spine. Finally he stuck his head out of the porthole and let the sea air strike his face. Down a little way the ship cutting through the sea made a steady, complaining noise. The stars all around him filled him with awe. Everything was so magnificent Standish felt like a little child.

Withdrawing his head from the porthole, Standish decided to get up and dress. He had shaved upon retiring and a bath could wait until after breakfast, before he went swimming in the pool. He would just get dressed and browse around and watch the sun come up.

Even on this informal ship Standish dressed decorously. Somehow, he felt he was not the man for slacks or outlandish sports costumes. All through the trip he had worn his conservative business suits. There were five in all, and after switching on the electric light Standish selected a gray from the spacious wardrobe trunk standing open in the corner. But first he stepped out of his pajamas and, standing in his bare skin, washed his teeth, hands, and face at the water basin in the room. Next he combed his straight, ruly, dull-black hair. When he was dressed he carefully removed his money, keys, and the wallet containing his papers from the brown suit he had worn the previous day and placed them inside the proper pockets of the gray.

Once out in the passageway, he got that feeling he was always getting aboard the *Arabella* of being an impish little boy engaged in some devilish business. The scene was so serene that the hum from the engine room made Standish shiver again. He walked almost on tiptoe, as if the clump of his shoes on the steel plates would be sacrilegious. The whole world was so quiet that Standish felt mystified. The lone ship plowing through the broad sea, the myriad of stars fading out of the wide heavens—these were all elemental things that both soothed and troubled Standish. It was as if he were learning for the first time that all the vexatious problems of his life were meaningless and unimportant; and yet he felt ashamed at having had them in the same world that could create such a scene as this.

Standish strolled into the empty saloon and served himself a cup of black coffee from the all-night percolator. He drank the coffee without sugar, letting the hot, bitter liquid arouse his inner body. Then he smoked his first cigarette, inhaling deeply. The sea air had done wonders for his health; the rasping smoker's cough he had had when he ran away from his wife several months ago had disappeared completely. Always a strong man who took excellent care of himself, Standish knew that now he was at his physical peak. He was thirty-five years old, and he had never felt better in his life.

It was nearly five o'clock, and the sun was about to rise. Standish tiptoed down to the well deck and sat for a few minutes on the damp tarpaulin covering the hatch. Then, feeling excited for no good reason, as he recalled vividly later on, he went through the fire door and along the 'tween-deck passageway, where the galley, the crew's mess, the stewards' quarters, and other such rooms were situated. The cook, an American Negro, was sleepily starting a fire in the galley stove.

Standish said good-morning, though he did not want to; human voices, including his own, made the scene less lovely. The cook grinned and returned the salutation, adding some cliché about Mr. Standish's being up early again this morning. "Ah, yes," Standish said, and he walked forward about twenty more yards. This was his favorite early-morning place aboard the *Arabella.* His favorite evening place was on the boat deck, behind a certain lifeboat, where he could sit alone and watch the sun go down in the gorgeous sky. But this morning spot was an ingeniously clever one. It was an opening in the *Arabella's* hull; the passageway turned a little, before continuing forward, to the extreme starboard, and then there were two sturdy fire doors which had more bolts than a treasury vault. Because the *Arabella* was sailing in such a calm sea, with good weather reports coming in over the wireless, these doors were open day and night. Here you were closest to the sea. You could hold on to one of the many brackets and lean far over and look down into the water. There was the Pacific Ocean not fifteen feet below, the sea at the *Arabella's* water line foaming and bubbling in different colors according to the time of the day. It made you slightly dizzy if you watched it too long, which was exactly what Standish did. That, however, was not the reason for Standish's misfortune. Normal in every way, Standish was not inclined to dizzy spells.

He stood there a long time, probably fifteen minutes, just listening to the melancholy bubbling of the water and the hum of the *Arabella's* engines, breathing quietly of the soft air and trying to follow with alert eyes the imperceptible blending of night into day. However, like many another thing, this was a pleasure a grown man tired of if he indulged himself too long. The thrill of being so dangerously close to the ocean palled on Standish after a while, making him feel slightly foolish. The reason he felt so foolish, he figured out many hours later, was that he was getting the thrill of a child, and all full-grown males resent that very much when they think about it at all.

Standish decided to desert this place, though he suddenly realized it would not be many more times he would stand here. Next week Balboa; then another ship where a man probably had to dress for dinner—en route to New York and the children and Olivia. He would have sat down on the deck for a while and hung his feet over the side of the *Arabella,* except that there were several grease spots around. The stewards dumped the refuse overboard from this place every night. Apparently they had been slovenly last night; there were some potato peelings and other bits of refuse on the deck, and they smelled a little, though not enough to spoil Standish's pleasure. Later in the day, Standish presumed, the sailors would swab the deck clean.

Clutching a secure bracket, Standish gazed for one long last time at the rising sun and the gentle ocean. He imagined he would never forget the poignancy of this moment. The world was filled with dignity. Dignity was what a man needed to live in peace.

Finally Standish wondered for no good reason about the surprising difference on this ocean between the dawn and the twilight. He decided to have another cup of coffee. He stepped back with his left foot and removed his hand from the bracket. When the sole of his left shoe moved backwards it hit a grease spot. Standish made a desperate move to grasp the bracket again and to hold the ground with his right foot. But he missed the bracket, and his right shoe hit into another grease spot, or perhaps it was the same one; Standish never found out. The grease spot was deceptive. It was coarse and gummy on top, and just looking at it you never would suspect it was dangerous. But apply pressure suddenly, as Standish had done, and you found yourself sliding on a surface as slippery as ice.

Two

Standish's first thought when he hit the water was to save himself from being mangled by the propeller. It was as if all his life he had studied exactly what to do in the event he fell overboard into the Pacific Ocean. The instinct of self-preservation raged strong in Standish's breast at this moment, and he did the right things. Many years back, when Standish was but a youth, the third officer of a passenger liner en route to France from New York had told him, in the course of an aimless conversation, that not so many men who fell overboard got mangled in propellers as the layman supposed. Standish had forgotten the third mate's name, but a few minutes later he was destined to conclude that, judging from his own experience, the fellow knew what he was talking about.

The *Arabella* was a single-screw ship, proceeding at the niggardly pace of ten knots. The sea was as calm as an artificial lake. Standish did a gawky, gangling straight dive into the brine. His arms went in first, then his head, and then the rest of his body, his feet doubling up awkwardly as he struck the Pacific Ocean.

Immediately he felt himself in an unfriendly whirlpool. The *Arabella* tried to pull Standish back to her broad bosom, and the sea tried to pull him away. Although his eyes were shut tight under the water, Standish instinctively kicked and flailed out in the right direction. Mastering all the force in his arms and biceps, he hurled his body up to the surface and away from the ship. Again the *Arabella* sucked at him like a gigantic magnet, and again he beat the foaming water furiously. The next moment he felt himself flung about with great force. "Oh, Lord!" Standish said to himself. "Oh, Lord!" He knew the *Arabella's* stern was abreast of him and an inner sense told him it was futile to struggle during the next few fateful moments. So he abandoned himself to his fate and felt himself describing several underwater somersaults and other acrobatic contortions against his will. How close he was drawn during these mad gyrations to the churning propeller of the *Arabella* Standish never discovered. Suddenly he felt himself buffeted mercilessly, as if two mammoth hands were slapping him back and forth between their palms. He was pushed so far down under the sea that his ears ached from the change of pressure. But otherwise he was unharmed. He held his breath throughout the ordeal, keeping his eyes and mouth clamped tight, and when he bobbed to the surface of the sea a moment later in the center of the *Arabella's* brackish wake, he had not even swallowed any water.

Standish's thoughts during these seconds were strangely enough more concerned with shame than with fear. Men of Henry Preston Standish's class did not go around falling off ships in the middle of the ocean; it just was not done, that was all. It was a stupid, childish, unmannerly thing to do, and if there had been anybody's pardon to beg, Standish would have begged it. People back in New York knew Standish was smooth. His upbringing and education had stressed smoothness. Even as an adolescent Standish had always done the right things. Without being at all snobbish or making a cult of manners Standish was really a gentleman, the good kind, the unobtrusive kind. Falling off a ship caused people a lot of bother. They had to throw out life preservers. The captain and chief engineer had to stop the ship and turn it around. A lifeboat had to be lowered; and then there would be the spectacle of Standish, all wet and bedraggled, being returned to the safety of the ship, with all the passengers lining the rail, smiling their encouragement and undoubtedly, later on, offering him innumerable anecdotes about similar mishaps. Falling off a ship was much worse than knocking over a waiter's tray or stepping on a lady's train. It was even more embarrassing than the fate of that unfortunate society girl in New York who tripped and fell down a whole flight of stairs while making her grand entrance on the night of her debut. It was humiliating, mortifying. You cursed yourself for being such a fool; you wanted to kick yourself. When you saw other men committing these wretched buffoons' mistakes you could not find it in your heart to forgive them; you had no pity on their discomfort.

Thoughts of this nature flashed through Standish's mind even while he was turning the rude somersaults under the water and coming God alone knew how close to the thrashing blades of the *Arabella's* propeller. Then, as he went shooting up to the surface of the sea, desperate for a breath of air, two new trends of thought dominated his brain. One was that he must instantly apprise the *Arabella* of his predicament. The other was that it was all hilariously funny—a man of his age falling off a ship.

However, the first idea was stronger than the second. When his head popped up out of the foaming water, he opened his mouth and took a deep breath. At the same time he started to shout his warning.

But no word came from his lips. Automatically treading water, Standish opened his eyes and looked upon the most terrifying sight he had ever seen; it was so terrifying it paralyzed his mind momentarily—not from fear, but from wonderment. It was the indecently broad and naked backside of the *Arabella,* staring at him ominously with its many porthole-eyes as it drew away from him in an ocean of froth. Standish had never imagined a ship, or anything else, could possibly look like that. In his travels he had become a connoisseur of the lines of ships; he knew a pretty one when he saw one. In Honolulu, looking at the *Arabella* from a distance as she lolled at her pier, he had admired her instantly. She was long and not too wide, had no incongruities of funnels or chimneys, was painted a modest gray, had a bridge that did not protrude, and a well deck that aided her to accomplish a graceful ending-off. The *Arabella* gave the impression of combined sturdiness and daintiness—in Honolulu. You thought of her as a "Miss"; a rather buxom Miss who knew her way about, but a Miss all the same.

But now Standish realized how greatly he had erred. His eyes bulged slightly in their sockets in those few moments as he stared, fascinated and horrified, at the revolting sight. Once at the zoo in New York he had seen the unadorned posterior of a full-grown baboon, and he had been fascinated for a while until his finer self got a grip on his coarser and he had turned away to look at the elephants. The *Arabella's* stern recalled to him the backside of that baboon. The propeller churning the water made a persistent "whooshing" sound the likes of which Standish had never heard anywhere before. From the poop deck, where those port-hole-eyes regarded him solemnly and eerily, the stern curved in and away down to the rudder, fairly proclaiming by the withdrawing lines that these were private parts from which a modest man should turn his eyes. Across the center, under the porthole-eyes, she had tattooed on the flesh in monstrously large letters:

ARABELLA—NEW YORK

If Standish had had his choice he would not have looked at that tattoo mark until he had lived with the *Arabella* for a good many years.

The *Arabella's* stern was so big, and he so small, that Standish was dumb. It was as if you were walking in Central Park, gazing up at the skyscraper apartments with their gold domes near by, and suddenly, rounding a clump of bushes, came face to face with a dinosaur with sprouting horns. You would be shocked out of your wits for a good many moments before your reflexes worked properly and you let out a yell. Many hours later Standish was to reason all this out and, though being unable to forgive himself for the lapse, come to an understanding with himself that it was inevitable.

The *Arabella* had advanced a good hundred yards meanwhile; thirty at least before Standish came to the surface, and seventy more while he stared speechless. Finally his mind came to the awful realization of those wasted seconds. He struggled furiously with himself to regain his composure, and that, perhaps, was his undoing. For he succeeded, after a tremendous exertion, in becoming a rational person again. If his horror had ascended into a state of extreme fear he would have shouted his head off for assistance; he would have raved and shrieked. And perhaps somebody aboard the *Arabella* would have heard his cries, though even that was doubtful, owing to peculiar circumstances in the forecastle of the ship at that time.

As it was, Standish was doomed by his breeding to be a gentleman even at this moment. The Standishes were not shouters; three generations of gentlemen had changed the trumpet in the early Standish larynx to a dulcet violoncello. It had not even been necessary to teach the boy Henry Preston Standish not to shout; he had known instinctively that a modified voice with a dignified tone was the Standish forte, one of the many subdued traits that enabled the Standishes to flourish in the cosmopolitan world.

So after becoming as rational as any gentleman could who had just fallen off a ship, Standish informed the *Arabella* of his indiscretion.

"Man overboard!" he shouted. "Man overboard!" Only he realized—and it struck him very funny—that he was not shouting. You would have to raise an awful outcry to make an impression on the Pacific Ocean, and Standish got the silly feeling he was only whispering.

"Man overboard!" he said a third time, straining extra hard to make his voice carry. But apparently the *Arabella* was indifferent to his plaint; her backside regarded the man in the ocean with an inscrutable visage.

"Hello there!" Standish said, watching the *Arabella* withdraw another ten, twenty, thirty; yards. "Hello there, I say! Man overboard, overboard, overboard! Hey!——Hey!"

Unconscious that one of her guests was floundering in the sea, the *Arabella* continued on her true course. Voices carried far on the quiet ocean, but there was something conspiring against Standish—a bit of human frailty in the forecastle of the *Arabella.*

There were two sections to the forecastle, one on the starboard, where the sailors slept; another on the portside for the firemen, oilers, and wipers. One of the sailors was a Finn named Bjorgstrom whom Standish had never met. Bjorgstrom was a good fellow with humble manners who would stand cap in hand before his superiors and smile nicely—when he was sober. But he did not understand that his race was not cut out for swilling and he had hidden in his locker some cheap okolehau which he had bought in Honolulu. All the previous evening, harboring some temporary grudge against life, he had sipped at the okolehau; and now the potent liquid had taken full effect. When Standish made his ineffectual bid for help, Bjorgstrom was raising a terrific rumpus in the forecastle of the *Arabella.* He had been singing and talking loudly to himself; and finally another sailor named Gaskin, who wished to catch some sleep, asked him to keep quiet. Bjorgstrom refused point-blank and became quite aggressive about it. One word led to another, and soon the two men nearly came to blows. Bjorgstrom's tongue being loosened by liquor and Gaskin's being naturally garrulous, a boisterous argument started that increased in pitch and volume with each passing moment. Although the passengers and the officers forward did not hear it, the crew in both sections of the forecastle did. The noise awakened all who were slumbering, and they added their irate cries to the maelstrom of sound, demanding absolute silence so that they could go back to sleep.

Soon an awful din of boos, catcalls, and full-throated voices reverberated through the steel-plated forecastle of the *Arabella.* During those anguished moments for Standish things finally reached such a stage that Bjorgstrom pulled a knife and Gaskin was forced to knock him unconscious by hitting him on the head with an old shoe. Bjorgstrom apologized to Gaskin later in the day, when he awoke after a long sleep, drank several quarts of water, and found himself sober again. The two men shook hands, slapped each other on the back, and they are friends to this day. However, one can understand that in all that din it was quite impossible to hear the meek voice of Standish crying in the water.

Standish, of course, was not aware of these circumstances. As the *Arabella* retreated further into the distance the thing happened to Standish that should have happened a few minutes back. He became aware of his fate, lost his reason, and regained his real voice. He let out such ferocious and terror-stricken shouts that the original Standish who settled on American soil around 1650 would have nodded approvingly could he have heard him in his grave.

"Man overboard!" Standish shouted. "Man overboard, man overboard, man overboard!"

Ten, twenty, thirty times Standish repeated the refrain until he was slightly blue in the face and his breath came in rasping pants. But the *Arabella* chose to be deaf as she continued on her way. The third mate was studying charts in the pilot house; the quartermaster was lost in a dream, his eyes on the compass and his hands lightly on the helm; Captain Bell was having coffee in his cabin, gazing proudly at his nearly completed four-masted schooner; the cook was rattling dishpans in the galley; and all the others were at work down below or else asleep.

Standish stopped his shouting as suddenly as he had started. The *Arabella* was now at least a quarter of a mile away. The wake in which Standish trod water mingled with and vanished into the sea. It was one thing to swim in the foaming wake and another to bob gently in the steady sea. One was ephemeral, part of the life that Standish knew, a thing created by something that was created by man. The other was eternal and incomprehensible. In the wake you were aware of your predicament as something temporary. But in the sea!...

Unaccountably; Standish began to laugh. It was difficult; he had to lie over on his back and look straight up at the dim sky, but he managed it. He laughed as he had never laughed before in his life, or would never again; roars of laughter, peals of laughter, laughter that made the tears roll out of his eyes and choked his throat. Henry Preston Standish falling off a ship! Henry Preston Standish alone in the middle of the ocean! It was truly funny; it was the marrow of all humor. If Olivia could see him now...the children!

The rising sun, which had been hidden from Standish since he fell overboard by the *Arabella's* steaming straight into it, all at once became visible on the horizon; either Standish had shifted slightly with the current or the *Arabella's* quartermaster had permitted the ship to go slightly off her compass course. Standish raised himself slightly in the water and laughed into the face of the rising sun. She had risen full and round in the low eastern sky; the bottom of her chin was just resting impatiently on the horizon. She stared at him imperiously, as if to demand who was this strange fish in her familiar sea.

And suddenly the real loneliness of his position dawned on Henry Preston Standish. He was such a puny bundle of life in such an immense world. The sun was so strong and he so weak.

This measureless ocean, so sure of its powers, reminded him he was just a frightened man far away from his home. Several moments passed before Standish realized he had stopped laughing.

Three

There was a narrow scar an inch long on the upper part of Standish's right wrist. That was where, seven years ago, Olivia had bitten him. Subsequently she had married him (giving the wound time to heal) and they were a happily wedded couple. Forces beyond Standish's control had given Olivia cause to bite him. He had met her at a dinner dance tendered by the honorable stock brokerage firm of Pym and Bingley, which later became known as Pym, Bingley, and Standish. Standish was a youngish man only five years out of Yale. Olivia was the niece of Pym, who was a brother-in-law of Bingley, and as soon as Standish set eyes on her those forces he was unable to control seized and shook him. It had been the same two or three times before in his childhood and youth when, for instance, he wished to go to Yale and his father had insisted on Princeton. Of course, his father had not bitten him, though Standish had his way and went to Yale.

Olivia bit him when Standish drove her home from the dance and tried to kiss her solemnly in the parked car. Later they discovered the only difference between a kiss and that kind of bite was the impermanence of the former. They were married within three months and in the course of the years had two children, whom they loved decently enough. Their lives were decorous, prim, and citified, with little to distinguish them from those of thousands of other well-to-do families living in four-room apartments on Central Park West. They never went hungry or thirsty and never encountered any vicissitude to make them sit up with a jolt and realize a grim kind of life was going on around them.

Standish's father and mother were living. They, too, were decent folk who resided in the Oranges, New Jersey. Standish was one of three children, the other two being girls, and he had had the best of everything without realizing it was the best; taking it all for granted in an unimaginative sort of way.

Those forces beyond control swayed Standish seldom in his life, but when they did they were all-powerful and he was a slave to their veriest whim. Otherwise life flowed on smoothly, hardly murmuring in his ears.

"Henry's the sad one in the family," his Aunt Clara,

who was his mother's sister, had once remarked in the course of a discussion of the Standish traits, vices, and virtues. What she meant was that Standish was by nature conservative. Breeding had taken the bright colors out of him, leaving him as uninteresting as a canvas in gray.

He did all the proper things, but without enthusiasm. He kept himself in fine trim by swimming and playing handball at the Athletic Club and golf in season with Pym and Bingley. He kept himself in funds by selling other people stocks and buying government bonds for himself. He was well informed and a good citizen. He voted carefully. He did everything carefully. His apartment was always in spotless array, his larder full. He drank moderately, smoked moderately, and made love to his wife moderately; in fact, Standish was one of the world's most boring men. Though psychologists may assert it is impossible, Standish was neither an introvert nor an extrovert.

Standish loved his children, Henry, Jr., five, and Helen, three, in a proud, melancholy sort of way.

There was never a breath of scandal connected with Standish, though he visited night clubs, often without Olivia, and played bridge and spent evenings at the club bar—moderately.

And yet one day in spring only three months ago, shortly after he had quietly celebrated his seventh wedding anniversary by taking Olivia and the Pyms and Bingleys to the theater, Standish, sitting in his private office downtown, suddenly found himself assailed by a vague unrest. He stopped what he was doing and looked around at familiar things, the papers on his desk, the windows, the pictures on the walls, the two telephones. All these appurtenances had always been desirable and comforting; but now, Standish realized in amazement, they were but dust in his mouth. He felt sick, tired, and depressed. Making suitable apologies to Pym and Bingley, who were too preoccupied with financial transactions to observe how serious was his affliction, he went for a long and lonely walk around Battery Park.

Standish had never before taken such a long and lonely walk. A veil lifted from before his eyes and he saw the world in different colors. The air he breathed smelled different; the cigarette he was smoking had a peculiar taste; there was a subtle buzzing going on in his head, the same head which had heretofore been one of the most level in the financial district.

In the park the waters of the bay lapped restlessly against the stone shorefront, and Standish leaned idly against a railing, looking out toward the sea with frightened, bloodshot eyes. Forces beyond his control grasped him and shook him by the shoulders, whispering between clenched teeth: *"You must go away from here, you must go away!"*

Where they wanted him to go, or why, Standish had no idea. He walked up Broadway. There was no sane reason why he must go away; everything was in its proper place in his life. Business was good. The children were growing and it was interesting sitting back and looking at them. Olivia was faithful to him; he would bet his last dollar on that; and she was one of those well-groomed women who would be attractive and beautiful for many years to come.

Standish returned to his office. The sight of Pym and Bingley actually sickened him. Fortunately, he left before they noted his disgust. He took a taxicab home and went straight to bed. Olivia wanted to call a doctor right away, but Standish said no, he merely wanted to rest alone in his bedroom. Olivia called the doctor anyway, and Standish was too preoccupied with his own thoughts to protest.

This room was a prison. The apartment, the office, Olivia, and the children were his keepers. He felt he had to escape, or he would go mad.

The doctor, a sensible family practitioner who had delivered the two Standish children, said nothing seriously was the matter with Standish; just weak from overwork, though his blood pressure was a little high. He advised Standish to stay in bed for several days and to try not to think too much about the brokerage business. He said it might be wise for Standish to go away somewhere for a rest, but Standish paid no attention to him.

Standish did not think about the brokerage business at all; he thought only that he never would be able to breathe freely again unless he went far away. Olivia was extremely nice and normal about the whole affair; it never even occurred to her Standish might be in need of a psychiatrist. Nervous and mental ailments were not in the Standish blood. She merely made certain the doctor came every day and nobody bothered her husband.

On the fourth day of his illness Standish looked at her with pitiful eyes.

"Olivia," he said, "I must go away."

She truly loved him. "Of course. How stupid of me not to see how badly you've been looking these last few months. You need a rest, Henry. Do you want to go to the mountains or to the sea?"

"The sea."

Standish got out of bed and dressed hastily and took a taxicab to a travel agency. Olivia did not ask to go along on the trip with him; she knew he wanted to go alone.

Standish bought a ticket on an American ship sailing the next day for California. Once on the West Coast, he could decide where to go next. It was agreed he would stay away two or three months. Standish found it difficult keeping his composure during those last twenty-four hours at home. He felt himself going to pieces, and being unable to offer Olivia a logical explanation made it worse. She was wonderful about it all; a different wife might have sought a hidden motive, business reverses she knew nothing about, perhaps, or another woman waiting for him somewhere. But Olivia was loyal and trusting to the end. When Standish kissed her good-by he felt ashamed because there was no fervor in that kiss; his mind was on far horizons and not on Olivia.

The children, too, seemed to understand they must not raise a fuss. Henry, Jr., gazed at his father appealingly and was mute when Standish kissed him hastily on the cheek. Even little Helen looked up at him from her crib with wondering, sad eyes.

When the warning whistle sounded on the ship, Olivia grasped her husband's right hand and gazed at him a long time with eyes full of compassion and tenderness.

"Take care, Henry," she said. "And make sure you have a long rest."

He averted his gaze, feeling miserable and in shackles. Muttering something about not failing to write her from every port, he escorted her to the gangplank.

He did not even stay to watch her standing in the crowd on the pier. Wondering what in God's name was the matter with him, he locked himself in his cabin and smoked an endless chain of cigarettes. He could feel the ship leaving the pier and proceeding down the harbor. He felt he was waiting for something, but did not know what.

For three hours he sat wretchedly in his cabin, and then suddenly he got up and without thinking or feeling any different he walked out into the passageway and up two flights of stairs to the deck.

When the wind smote his face, the shock of exultation was so great that he tottered weakly to the rail and held on for dear life. The ship was past Ambrose

Lightship, and all his weariness, all his doubts and fears, vanished magically into the sea. His heart beat wildly for joy. Yet he realized that although he felt good again it was not the same way he had felt before.

Standish went into the library and wrote Olivia a long letter about the good effects of the sea air.

The trip to California was delightful. It seemed he had time for everything: reading, writing, playing, eating, drinking, and sleeping. But there was a certain zest to these things now that he had not experienced back home before; all his sensations were intensified.

When Standish reached San Francisco he took a leisurely voyage up the coast and through the inland water route to Alaska. He made friends wherever he went, but though everybody was fond of him he preferred to be alone most of the time. Back in San Francisco he toyed with the idea of returning to New York; in fact, he spoke to Olivia over the long-distance telephone one night. As soon as he heard her voice he dropped the idea of returning.

"It's awfully lonely without you here, Henry," Olivia said. "Can't you come back?"

"I'd like to see Honolulu as long as I'm out this way," he said out of a clear sky. "I probably Won't be able to take a trip like this for a long time to come."

He asked her how the children were, and she said they had been moody and fretful since he left. "They miss you, Henry. Really they do." He almost stamped his foot. "I'd like to go to Hawaii."

Then her voice was frightened three thousand miles away. "Why, Henry?"

"I don't know."

"Henry! What's happened?"

He reassured her. "Nothing, Olivia, honestly. I feel fine. I've gained weight and I've never felt stronger in my life."

When he said good-by and hung up the receiver he felt foolish. A man of his age, thirty-five, in the prime of life; a successful, hardheaded broker giving in to his moods this way! It was stupid. But when he bought his steamship ticket for Hawaii he actually felt merry. That trip, too, was pleasant all the way. He stayed at Waikiki for three days and then decided to go home. It was purely by accident that he took the *Arabella,* he had planned to return to San Francisco on the same ship that had brought him to Honolulu, and then fly back to New York. But when he went down from his room for dinner and stopped at the desk to put his key in the box he overheard the assistant manager telling a strange man—Standish never was able to bring back to his mind's eye the picture of this man—about the *Arabella.*

"If you want a nice rest," the assistant manager was saying, "why don't you take the *Arabella* tomorrow? Twenty-one days to Panama, and all smooth sailing."

The strange man told the assistant manager twenty-one days were four too many for his purposes; he would take the usual ship back to San Francisco. But Standish walked moodily into the dining room, rolling the word *Arabella* around his tongue. He recalled that on the ship from New York to San Francisco, after they had cleared the Panama Canal, one of the passengers had told him about that trip. "If you want to see the most beautiful sunsets in the world on a sea unbelievably calm," the passenger had said, "take a ship from Panama to Hawaii, or return."

Standish made up his mind. There was no trouble getting reservations. He cabled Olivia. Instead of coming home in six days it would be another month. He sailed the next day aboard the *Arabella,* and never regretted his decision—until the thirteenth day out.

The point where Standish fell overboard was approximately North Latitude 12, West Longitude 108, in the Pacific Ocean.

Four

Those first few minutes of looking at the sun were bad minutes, but then the man that had been bred in Standish reasserted himself. The sun indeed was a terrifying and majestic spectacle, but after all it was only the sun, and the ocean only the ocean. This was the most peaceful stretch of ocean in the world; he was a strong man and it cost hardly any effort treading water and keeping afloat. Mr. Prisk several days ago had gone into a rather lengthy declamation to explain there were no sharks or dangerous fish in these waters. The reason had been lost on Standish; it was too nautical, having something to do with currents, the winds, and the temperature of the water, but the conclusion had remained in his mind and was one of the first things he thought about after the *Arabella* drew some distance away.

The sun was just up; a whole twelve hours stretched before Standish ere the sun would go down, and he was a conspicuous spot, he felt certain, on the serene sea. The temperature of the water approached lukewarm and the air held no chill. There would be no hardship in going any number of hours without food, and as for water, Standish, not yet feeling the pangs of thirst, was confident he could go twelve hours if necessary without a drink. Sooner or later his absence aboard the *Arabella* would be noticed; they would deduce instantly he had fallen overboard and would turn the ship around to search for him. And they could not help but find him in the broad daylight, unless they were totally blind; for he was the only flaw in the measureless sea. Somewhere in the back of his mind was the thought that the current must be moving him imperceptibly off the spot in the sea where the *Arabella* had dropped him, but he decided that this was nothing to worry about; if the current moved him it moved the *Arabella,* too, so things were even in the long run.

As a matter of fact, after a while Standish actually felt merry. Once long ago he had swum dangerously beyond the float at a Long Island beach and had suddenly felt merry. That was the way he felt now. There was no question about this being a terrific adventure; here he was, a broker of ordinary strength and talents, matching his wits against the elements. Even though the elements were inclined to be peaceful this was tremendously exciting. Standish could hardly wait until he would be able to tell somebody about it.

Facing the sun, even though it burned into his eyes, Standish thought about that subject at length, while he watched carefully to see when the *Arabella* would discover his absence and turn about to pick him up. Of course, there would be the disgrace he would have to face when he, a grown man apparently in full control of his senses, was hauled back aboard the *Arabella*; probably they even would have to launch a lifeboat to retrieve him. There would be the shame of explaining to Captain Bell, who undoubtedly would put all the blame on Mr. Prisk, according to the ancient maritime custom of blaming the first mate for everything. There would be the humiliation of facing the passengers, especially Mr. and Mrs. Brown, who would certainly think him a fool. And there would be the chagrin of being unable to prevent Mrs. Benson's children from speaking openly about the unhappy affair after the others would begin to understand, from a certain reserve that would be in his manner, that the subject was best not discussed unless he brought it up himself.

But after the trip was ended, when he returned to Olivia and the two children in New York, it would be pleasant to recount the sensations he was now experiencing. Pym and Bingley would be aghast.

Standish, treading water even more lazily than

before, smiled happily and soon found himself actually giggling like a hysterical child.

He could visualize Pym eyeing him askance. *"But weren't you afraid of the sharks?"*

"No, Pym. You see, there are no sharks in those waters. It has something to do with the current and the wind. It's too technical, or I'd try to explain."

Perhaps it might even be wiser to lie a bit on this point. After all, few persons ever spent time alone in the middle of the ocean, and nobody would be able to check up on him; nobody at least in his limited circle of businessmen and their wives.

"Of course I wasn't afraid of sharks, Pym old boy. When your time comes it comes, was the way I figured. If a shark was destined to find me he would have found me. That's what I said to myself, and let it go at that."

But Olivia. She was the one he wanted to tell the story to! Her blue eyes would be wide, and she would not interrupt while he spoke. That was one of the lovely things about Olivia; she never interrupted.

"There I was, darling, walking around the ship, and suddenly I got the idea to go down to a little opening on the lower deck and see the sun come up. I watched the sun for a while and then, stepping back, slipped and did a crazy dive straight into the ocean. Can you picture that? A man of my age! No, I wasn't scared. Why should I be scared? I'm a good swimmer, and the water was calmer than you can possibly imagine. I was excited, of course, and very interested in the

whole business. You see, there I was in one world on the ship? safe, secure, well fed, and presto!—a slip of the foot and I am in a totally different world a few seconds later."

Gloom suddenly came into Standish's mind. He observed that his moods were changing rapidly. Maybe he should not have thought about those two different worlds separated by a few seconds of time.

Standish automatically looked at his wrist watch. It was an expensive watch. His mother had given it to him when he was in college and he never had had any trouble with it. It kept excellent time and never needed repair. It probably cost a hundred dollars. But how quickly it had died the moment it hit the water! Put all things together and some are peculiarly fitted for life on land, while others thrive on water. A wrist watch gave up the ghost in a twinkling; water was its potent poison; a few drops of water and all breath was crushed out of it. Other things, rubber ducks, sponges, and seaweed, blossomed and grew fat on water. But what about a human being? Standish decided a human being was temperamental about water; sometimes he thrived on it and sometimes he withered.

The hands of the watch pointed to twenty-three minutes past five. He had turned the hands every day to correspond with the meridian time posted on the saloon bulletin board by Mr. Prisk. Twenty-three minutes after five was the exact time he fell overboard.

"It was exactly twenty-three minutes past five. I know,

you see, because my watch stopped when I hit the water."

Suddenly Standish felt impatient. He was not a man to tolerate impatience, as the clerks in the brokerage office knew very well. Why was the *Arabella* not turning around to pick him up so that he could start telling the story to somebody? It was lonely out here in the middle of the ocean. Why, if things went on this way he would end up by talking to himself, and that was something Henry Preston Standish could truthfully boast he had never done.

The *Arabella* was now only as big as a rowboat. Standish judged it was five miles away, and estimated he had been in the water about half an hour. In reality Standish had been in the water forty minutes and the *Arabella* was seven miles away. However, this error of judgment was due as much to his lack of experience in measuring time and distance as to his excusable optimism in the matter.

Treading water without any respite was becoming a bit of a strain. Standish remembered that he was buoyant. As a youth he had always thought that a funny word. A lifeguard had once explained it to him: "Some people are buoyant and some just ain't, that's all." Standish could stretch out his arms, point his toes, and, lying supine, arch his back. Then, if he kept his lungs filled with air, changing the supply in quick, cunning spurts, he could float endlessly without any great exertion. In his youth this had been one of his greatest delights, to swim several hundred yards out into Long Island Sound, shut his eyes, and just float in the water for maybe thirty minutes or an hour.

Standish decided to take advantage of his buoyancy. There was the problem of his clothes, but he would have to face it bravely. A stranger looking at Standish would have been willing to take a solemn oath that he wore white undergarments. But the truth of the matter was that Standish went in for stripes and colors. At present he wore a white athletic shirt and blue-and-yellow striped trunks. Besides the reason of natural male modesty, this was another reason why Standish had decided he would be damned before he would permit himself to be rescued stripped down to his underwear. Being taken aboard the *Arabella* in white trunks would be bad enough, but blue-and-yellow which all, including Mr. and Mrs. Brown, could appraise was impossible. A man's sense of decency was as important as his life.

The next minute Standish realized how untrue was that belief. He was getting a slight pain in his shoulders from treading water. As soon as he became aware of the strain he changed his mind. It never occurred to him that his mind was a plaything of his physical self; that convictions were all right until the body had some need, and then the body twisted the mind to do its bidding. All Standish knew was that suddenly he did not care if the good people aboard the *Arabella* saw his blue-and-yellow trunks. He wanted to float and, by God, he would.

He went about his preparations for undressing methodically. First he removed his shoes. He was able to get them off without untying the shoestrings; a little pressure and they came free. He let them move out of his sight in the ocean without even looking at them for one last time and only with the thought that they had cost thirty dollars and it was a good thing the bootmaker in New York had his measurements and could make him another pair in three days. Anyway, there were two more pairs aboard the *Arabella.*

Standish was no fool; important persons in the financial district would have told you, if Standish's name came up, that he was no fool.

It came to his mind that in this calm, gentle ocean there was one lurking peril—sunstroke—even though all of him except his head was under water. He must protect his head at all costs.

Standish's socks saved the day. Ducking under the water, he freed one from its garter and pulled it off his foot. Kipping it slightly, he was able to squeeze it down securely over his head. He repeated the process with the other sock. Now he had double protection against the sun even though, he thought wistfully, his present headgear would have caused much comment, mostly unfavorable, in the financial district. But nobody would ever see him this way except God and a couple of fish; he would pull it off his head when the *Arabella* came close.

All this while Standish realized he was trying to

delay the inevitable removal of his coat, vest, and trousers. It was not so much the pride he took in his suit as the things the pockets contained. But he decided that problem could be solved without any great difficulty. He would remove everything from his pockets and place the various objects inside his water-soaked wallet. And then he could hold on to the wallet or, better still, tie it on to his blue-and-yellow trunks. There was an adjustment loop in the back of his trunks under which he could securely hold the wallet.

Standish looked at the *Arabella* in the distance. She was no bigger than a canoe. He looked at the sky. It was as great as a man's courage, and the sea stretched out wider than his hopes. The water, seen from the *Arabella's* 'tween-deck passageway, had seemed bluish-gray, but now that he was in it and the day was older it was bluish-green.

Standish took out his wallet. With some difficulty he inspected its contents; he could not resist the curiosity. Holding the wallet at arm's length and keeping afloat at the same time was a great strain, but it was worth the effort.

In one of the wallet pockets, neatly kept together by a rubber band, was a batch of old speakeasy cards. These had been absolutely useless for a great many years in New York; Standish never knew why he had carried them around so long, except, perhaps, that he had done a major part of his courting of Olivia in those delightfully secret drinking places. But if they had been useless in New York, how doubly useless they were in the middle of the Pacific! Standish racked his brain to think of something more useless in his present situation, but decided after a few moments that that was an impossible task.

Other papers in the wallet were equally interesting. The five hundred dollars in traveler's checks were water-soaked, but no doubt the bank had provisions to redeem them. After he explained the reason for getting them wet he imagined there would be no difficulty in getting new ones. The little address book which he had kept for five years would be a great loss if its pages were made illegible; it would take him many months to get up a new one. The membership cards in the Finance Club, Athletic Club, Weebonnick Golf Club, and Yale Club created no problem; after learning of his odd experience the directors of the various enterprises no doubt would be happy to give him gilt-edged cards in place of the old ones.

But that snapshot of Olivia, himself, and the children which his mother had taken the last time they had visited the Oranges—that was almost five months ago—troubled Standish. He looked at it a long time and tried to brush the water off it. He wondered what they all were doing at the moment so far away on dry land.

Included among the effects of the wallet was an old rent receipt, several scraps of paper he could not account for, and a book of three-cent stamps. Standish did not think about these things too long. He removed his keys, money, fountain pen, comb, nail file, and reading glasses from the various pockets of his coat, vest, and trousers and carefully placed them inside the wallet. Then, with a sigh of relief, firmly clutching the wallet in his right hand, he slipped out of his coat. He unbuttoned his vest and got rid of that garment. He slipped his braces off his shoulders and wriggled out of his trousers. The trousers floated away immediately, but the coat and vest bobbed near by for a while before going away. Standish finally ripped off his shirt, a piece of good white English broadcloth, and cast it away from him.

He was a little tired from all the exertion, but when he secured the wallet in the loop of his trunks and then lay back, as he had done as a youth, his strength came back quickly. He breathed regularly, filling his lungs with the clean, dustless air. There was no fear in his mind, or any sense of worry over his predicament, only a feeling of wonderment at the vastness of things. It troubled him a bit that the *Arabella* had not turned around as yet; it was no bigger than a barrel now; but he felt certain it would do so at any moment. Standish lay inert in the water, gently bobbing in the negligible swell. He felt very comfortable.

"I got the most astounding sense of well-being lying there in the middle of the ocean. Altogether different, Olivia, from swimming close to shore. I don't know how to describe it; I sort of felt I was the last person in the world. It was thrilling, really it was, watching that ship going further

and further away, not really knowing whether it was ever going to come back for me. I can't begin to describe to you the vastness of things out there, the bigness, the immensity of the water and the sun and the sky."

Somehow there came into Standish's mind the words of an old song as he had sung it in school days. He did not sing the song now; he merely hummed the tune, but the words were in his mind:

My grandfather's clock was too large for the shelf,
So it stood ninety years on the floor;
It was taller by half than the old man himself,
Though it weighed not a pennyweight more.

It was bought out of pawn
On the day that he was born,
And was always his treasure and pride;
But it stopped
Short
Never to go again
When the old...man...died.

Five

Standish, floating in the water, concentrated his thoughts on the people aboard the *Arabella* and as a result fell into the common error of believing the converse was true. But the truth of the matter was that the good people aboard the *Arabella* hardly thought of Standish at all.

The Negro cook, in whom flowed an elemental desire to be kind, was the last person to see Standish; after saying good-morning to him as he had paused in the passageway the cook went back to his task of preparing the day's fare. With the exercise of just a little logic the cook could have deduced something was amiss, and yet he did not. It was a matter of eggs. Breakfast was served from eight to nine-thirty, but everybody was always in the saloon at eight sharp. Standish was a poached-egg man; his father had been one and so had his father's father. Not only was Standish a poached-egg man; he was the only poached-egg man aboard the *Arabella.* The first breakfast out, when Standish had ordered poached eggs, the cook had done some muttering; there was no egg poacher aboard and he had to do the business in a shallow frying pan. But later on, after talking to Standish and finding him a pleasant man, the cook really did not mind. On this morning Standish ordered no eggs. The cook, however, poached them at ten minutes past eight and put them in the oven to keep warm until the steward would bring them up to the saloon with the other orders. The steward, who really was not a very bright fellow, owing to a combination of youthful environment and ancient heritage, declined to take them, mumbling something about Standish not yet being up for breakfast. Somehow, the cook saw no significance in that slurred statement. His mind should have worked furiously; he should have known Standish was a methodical man who always ate breakfast at the same hour. But the fact remained that he did not think of this. Furthermore, he felt no great remorse over the waste of the eggs; they belonged to the *Arabella* and it was nothing out of his pocket. There was no way of checking further; the rest of the food was served in community. The cook decided, somewhere way in the back of his mind, that Standish had been late for breakfast and had gone without his poached eggs. Around ten o'clock the cook threw the eggs along with other rubbish into the ocean from the same spot where fate had jettisoned Standish.

The passengers assembled for breakfast were concentrating all their attention on the inner rumblings of their respective stomachs. Mrs. Benson, of course, was not thinking of Standish; Standish himself, could he have been asked, would have said it was unreasonable to expect Mrs. Benson to think of him. Feeding four young children orange juice, oatmeal, eggs, and milk was a herculean task, even with a steward near by to assist. If Mrs. Benson was thinking at all she was thinking how nice it would be to settle down in Panama with Mr. Benson in a house where some sort of routine could be established for the children.

Little Jimmy was so troublesome on this morning that Mrs. Benson finally gave up trying to make him eat his oatmeal. But being a wise and stern mother, she punished him by confining him to his cabin for one hour after breakfast. This was indeed unfortunate, for it was Jimmy's custom to search out Standish every morning after breakfast and ask him to play, a request which Standish had never refused, though somehow he had always got out of actually engaging in the lad's strenuous games. Jimmy went immediately to his cabin at his mother's command and started to sulk. In the manner of a child, he permitted the punishment to grow in his mind. After an hour he began to like it. He stayed in the cabin for two hours, thinking of ways to torture his mother; and when she finally came and dragged him out by brute force, he was such an impossibly hurt child looking for sympathy that he became grimly silent. He refused to play with any of the other children and spent the next hour going around biting his lips and looking so sickly pale and miserable that Mr. Travis, the chief engineer, who happened to come upon him in the passageway, felt sorry for him. "Top of the morning to you, my little man," Mr. Travis said, but when Jimmy, who had grown up in the flowering tranquillity of Honolulu's suburbs, replied succinctly: "Nuts," Mr. Travis understood the depths of the lad's suffering, for he, too, had led an unhappy life. "How would you like to be chief engineer for a while and run the ship?" Mr. Travis said, not at all taken aback by Jimmy's unmannerly retort. Standish would have acknowledged, if the question could have been put to him, that, taking into account Jimmy's temper, background, and age, there was naught for the boy to do but snap suddenly out of his doldrums, flash a broad smile, take Mr. Travis's sturdy hand, and trip blithely down the oily steps into the bowels of the ship. There Jimmy spent the two most delightful hours of his young life, and his mind was so occupied with wheels, gauges, and gadgets when he finally came up above that he never thought of Standish for the rest of the day.

Old Nat Adams came closer than any of the others to discovering Standish's absence 3 the only thing that prevented it was Nat's realization he was a man of the soil whereas Standish was a cosmopolitan gentleman. From the very start the two men had formed a friendship which flowered into a wistful brotherhood, due largely to a certain shyness and reserve in the makeup of each. Standish saw in this gnarled New England farmer the independence of spirit and simplicity of mind of his own forbears. And Nat looked upon Standish with respect, seeing a picture of the great, stylish city with all its urbanities and graces. He felt proud that Standish found so much in common with him, for he secretly believed they were as far apart as the poles. On the first day out Nat had wanted to strike up a conversation with Standish; just looking at him, dressed in his conservative business suit that whispered its exclusive tailoring, interested and excited the old farmer. That was why he was traveling around aimlessly, to meet gentlemen like Standish, talk with them, and learn from them how the world got on outside of New England's farmlands. But Nat knew from the very start that he could not go to Standish; Standish must come to him. And that was exactly what Standish did; finding an urbane excuse, he broke the ice, and the two became fast friends. For eleven days they were together, with Standish listening mostly, and always finding the old farmer's talk refreshing. But Standish always went to Nat and Nat understood that outside of New England's rural districts Standish was the superior man. Then, on the twelfth night out, which was the night preceding the morning of Standish's accident, Nat stood on the well deck all alone gazing at the evening stars and suddenly found a magnificently clever thought trailing through his mind. He would not return to New England by ship, as he had planned, but, when the *Arabella* reached Panama, would travel through Central America by auto, all the way up through Mexico, and then from Texas to New England by train. It was only half-past seven and Nat felt he had to tell somebody about this idea; it was too good to keep to himself. So on the spur of the moment he sought out Standish, though in the back of his mind there was still a certain reticence. Standish was in his cabin, writing a letter to Olivia, which he intended to send to New York by air mail from Panama. Nat knocked on the door and immediately felt sorry he had done so. But when Standish opened the door and saw who it was, most of Nat's doubts vanished. Standish was truly glad to see Nat; he invited him in and made him sit down and listened attentively while Nat expounded his new plans. Standish smiled enviously at the happy farmer; he told Nat he did not know much about transportation through Central America but imagined roads were scarce and the trip would be difficult. Standish said it might even be dangerous, but Nat laughed and asked: "Who would want to hurt an old man like me?" They talked for at least half an hour, and then Nat apologized for breaking in on Standish without an invitation and, against Standish's sincere protests, said goodnight and went away. But Nat thought about the trip all night; he did not sleep at all; just shut his eyes and dreamed pleasantly about verdant fields, natives with outlandish costumes, and hot-tasting foods. Toward dawn Nat dozed, but when he awoke at seven-thirty he was eager to talk to Standish again about the trip. New ideas had come into his head during the night; he might even hire a guide and a horse and carriage and go bouncing through Latin America that way. Nat Adams knew something about handling horses; it could well be done. It was a bitter disappointment not to see Standish at the breakfast table. After his hearty breakfast Nat paced back and forth on the boat deck. Finally he felt he must see Standish. He looked all over the ship for him and at last made up his mind to knock on his cabin door. He stood in front of the door for a long moment, his fist upraised and ready to strike. But then a sense of shame overwhelmed the good New England farmer. What gall he had, annoying Standish! Standish was asleep and here he was planning to wake him. Why did he not mind his own business, as he had always done, and stop bothering strangers? Nat walked away on tiptoe, his tongue between his false teeth. He borrowed a map of Central America from the third mate, retired to the privacy of his own cabin, and drew on the map thin pencil lines of a journey he never took. Later he erased the lines, for the map did not belong to him. At lunch he was really glad Standish was not in the saloon, for Nat had decided that Standish considered him an awful pest and put up so patiently with his childish chatter only because he was such a gentleman.

It was the same with the others; everybody thought Standish was someplace else aboard the ship without really thinking about him. Could Standish have chosen from the group one person to be especially angry at, the steward would have won the doubtful honor. This same steward who had told the cook Standish was not yet ready for his poached eggs had the duty of cleaning the passengers' cabins. What he lacked in wisdom he made up in a stubborn ability to do a drudge's work. Arriving at the door of Standish's cabin around ten o'clock, he knocked automatically, in the event Standish should still be in. Finding Standish was not in, as usual, he entered ceremoniously and started giving the room its customary cleaning. It never entered his mind that Standish's absence from both his room and the breakfast table meant something was wrong. The day being a Wednesday, the steward changed the bedsheets and pillowcases. When the bed was made with its clean linen, the ashtrays emptied, and the corners of the room dusted, the steward filled the water pitcher, put a fresh bar of soap atop the water basin and clean towels on the rack. Then he picked up the brown suit which Standish had left lying on the chair, brushed it carefully, and placed it back on its hanger in the steamer trunk, which was partly open. The soiled shirt, undergarments, and handkerchiefs which also lay on the chair he placed in the bottom drawer of the trunk. There was a cravat lying on the chair-shoulder, a conservative blue cravat with white polka dots. The steward eyed the tie cunningly, but finally sighed softly and, grasping it lightly between thumb and forefinger so as not to soil it, placed it back on its proper rack in the trunk. Finally his eyes roved the room and he decided with a doltish sense of self-satisfaction that it was really spick and span; no tenant could desire better service, unless he was a crank. He walked out softly, shutting the door lightly behind him, and went into Nat Adams's room, but found him sitting dreamily in a chair, drawing strange lines on a map.

An odd occurrence was a chance meeting between Mrs. Benson and Mr. and Mrs. Brown about two hours after breakfast. Mrs. Benson was an ardent habitude of the *Arabella's* swimming pool, and so was Standish. But Mr. and Mrs. Brown had their own idea about swimming and washing, believing the latter something to do between a locked door and a glazed window, and the former a stock in trade for persons in certain forms of commercial enterprise, such as pearl diving. Especially they detested the modern bathing suit, and most especially the red one worn with flaming scorn for the old conventions by Mrs. Benson.

Indignation rankled in their respective breasts whenever they saw it, for seeing it when it was within their range was unavoidable.

On this morning Mrs. Benson slipped out of her clothes and into her bathing suit promptly at ten and walked sans robe merrily to the swimming pool. She was quite disappointed to find Standish was not there; he had always been in the pool by ten on preceding days. After plunging in and swimming around alone for twenty minutes she suddenly spied Mr. and Mrs. Brown sitting together on deck chairs on the promenade deck. Mr. and Mrs. Brown were sharing an old Christian Science Monitor and trying their hardest not to think about Mrs. Benson's bathing suit. But Mrs. Benson had not the slightest idea she was displeasing them. On the spur of the moment she climbed out of the pool and, dripping wet, ran over to Mr. and Mrs. Brown.

"Have you seen Mr. Standish anywhere around?" she asked.

Mr. and Mrs. Brown eyed her askance. The water dripping down her thighs formed a pool at her feet, and the wet bathing suit clung to her skin to accentuate a feminine figure of which both Mrs. Benson and the absent Mr. Benson were justly proud. Years of missionary work among the Chinese had taught Mr. and Mrs. Brown to swallow their displeasure in the face of unpleasant incidents. So Mrs. Brown gazed at Mrs. Benson with a face expressing nothing, and Mr. Brown with eyes trying not to see too closely what none could escape who faced Mrs. Benson in her bathing suit.

The next moment Mr. Brown was saying: "I believe I saw him a while ago in the library."

When Mr. and Mrs. Brown secretly analyzed this statement later on they decided Mr. Brown had committed an error and had mistaken Nat Adams in the reading room for Standish. Never, not even to themselves, would Mr. and Mrs. Brown admit the statement was a complete fabrication invented for the sole purpose of getting rid of Mrs. Benson.

Mrs. Benson started out to look into the reading room, which was in a corner of the saloon, but just at that moment little Gladys came tripping down the passageway in her child's bathing suit, which also was red, shrieking she wanted to learn how to swim, so Mrs. Benson returned to the pool with her daughter. Later on she looked into the library, but Standish was not there.

The day wore on into an afternoon blessed by a sky surpassing for brilliant coloration any that had come before on the trip. The passengers assembled singly or in pairs for lunch, ate it, and dispersed for pleasant siestas or some quiet reading. Around three o'clock Mr. Prisk grew uneasy. There was nothing he could put his finger on, but he knew something was wrong. For a long while he stood alone on the boat deck and wondered what was the matter. All of a sudden Standish's name popped into his head. He realized he had not seen

Standish all day; neither at breakfast nor lunch, nor anywhere else on the ship. Immediately he got a hunch Standish had disappeared. Carefully he reasoned it out. Why should Standish's name pop into his head for no reason? There was a reason for everything, as every man of the sea knew from experience. It mattered not how the name popped into his head—whether it was by accident or divine intent or an explosion of accumulated intuitions; the fact was that the name had popped.

Mr. Prisk was a careful man in all things. Systematically he started a search, for there was nothing Mr. Prisk disliked more than to go bothering Captain Bell with false reports. He decided to spend at least an hour trying to prove to his complete satisfaction that Standish had not disappeared; if he would finally become convinced that the facts pointed to the opposite conclusion he would then reluctantly bring the news to the skipper. First Mr. Prisk looked inside Standish's cabin. Then he searched the *Arabella* from stem to stern in such a way that Standish could not pass him, if he were aboard, during that time. Then he questioned all the passengers separately (except Mr. and Mrs. Brown, who had to be questioned together) without creating any undue excitement or letting them know what he now was beginning to suspect. All admitted, except Mr. Brown, that they had not seen Standish since the previous evening. Mr. Brown said: "I believe I saw him in the reading room around nine-thirty, or was it Mr.

Adams?" Mr. Prisk ascertained it was Mr. Adams. Then he questioned the officers and crew, waking those who were asleep. He finally learned that the cook had spoken to Standish just before sunrise. Mr. Prisk walked down the passageway and stood for a long moment at the open door whose threshold Standish had unwillingly crossed. Finally Mr. Prisk sadly shook his head and sighed. This would mean endless trouble. But he tightened his jaw. A family man had to be humble at times; he was not the only family man in the world to eat dirt.

Captain Bell was sandpapering his four-masted schooner when Mr. Prisk came in.

"What is it, Prisk?" he asked without looking up.

"A man is missing, Captain—Mr. Standish, one of the passengers."

Captain Bell stopped his sandpapering. "What do you mean, missing!"

"As far as I can make out he hasn't been seen since five o'clock this morning."

"Five o'clock! What are you prattling about? That's ten hours!"

"I know, Captain."

"Search the ship."

"I did."

"Did you question everybody?"

"Yes, Captain."

Captain Bell put down the sandpaper angrily. "Ridiculous. He's probably down in the engine room somewhere. Damn it, Prisk, why come bothering me with these stupid reports? Oh, well, come along. I guess *I'll* have to search the ship and find him."

Six

The *Arabella* was growing smaller and smaller in the distance and Standish suddenly experienced a sinking feeling in his heart. This angered him, for whenever he had come across that phrase in a story book he had sniffed and blamed the author for a slovenly bit of description. But the fact remained, as he was forced to admit to himself, that whatever it was that made up the inside of his heart felt all at once as if it was sinking to a point around where his stomach was situated.

Not that he was smitten with any overpowering fear; he laughed brusquely at that idea. He felt he could last for hours, which he was certain would not be necessary. But every once in a while he found himself thinking: *"Courage, man, courage!"*

These spasms of internal whispering finally made Standish furious at himself. Of all the idiotic tricks since time began, he decided rather heatedly, falling off a ship into the middle of the ocean was by far the most colossal. It was so stupid, so absolutely without reason or precedent, so out of place for a man of his position! For a while Standish gnashed his teeth in an impotent rage. Nobody who knew him would ever expect him to do such a thing. His Aunt Clara would declare it an utter improbability. If his family, which included some wild specimens of men and women who had too much money and leisure, had gathered together and held a vote on who among them was most likely to fall off a boat, no one would have voted for him. And now here he was in this impossible predicament, and the *Arabella* drawing further and further away.

As suddenly as the rage assailed him it left him, and in its place came a sophisticated and rather unreasonable pose of resignation. Here he was in the middle of the brine and he would have to make the best of it until he was rescued; no sense wasting his strength cursing his fate.

And if he was not rescued—he looked again and saw the *Arabella* was a tiny speck on the sea—he would drown. For the first time, Standish considered in detail the problem of drowning. To start with, he considered the possibilities of not being rescued. He decided they were fair. Then he thought that if he was fated to drown he would drown; that was all. It was very simple and there was no sense getting melodramatic about it and beating his breast in a futile protest. It would not be so terrible to drown if a man went about it sensibly, without losing his head; and after he was dead the pain would be all over. Of course, he did not want to drown; there were so many things he wanted to live for. For all he knew, he was drowning right this minute; if the *Arabella* never turned around to fetch him this could really be said to be so. Standish shut his eyes and held his breath. According to everything he had read and been told, a drowning man saw his whole life pass before him in retrospect. Standish waited patiently for something to happen, but was unable to coax a single incident out of his past. It made him a little angry to see nothing in retrospect; after all, he was a normal man, and if other normal men saw things in retrospect he wanted to see them, too. But the next moment it made him happy. That probably meant he was not drowning—of course he was not drowning!

Standish looked carefully at the monotonous sky. The name of the Scandinavian freighter that had passed the *Arabella* going the other way to Hawaii suddenly came to his mind. It was amazing how that happened; he had not been thinking even remotely about the freighter, and now here it was in his brain, forgotten name and all. Ingrid, that was it. Perhaps the Ingrid would rescue him if the *Arabella* did not. But he knew there was no chance at all of that happening, and suddenly he found himself thinking: *"Standish...Standish... don't beguile yourself with idle hopes."* And now he was unhappy again.

He thought about the passengers on the *Arabella,* surely they were observing his absence. The cook had seen him go down the passageway and had not seen him return; the cook surely would report him missing. The steward would observe he did not order any breakfast—the steward would see he was not in his cabin; surely he would see it. And old Nat Adams—there was a certainty! If he doubted all the rest he could depend upon Nat. Nat probably was looking for him right this minute and getting good and worried, too. Any moment now Nat would report his absence to Mr. Prisk. And then they would have to turn the ship around to search for him. It was an unwritten law of the sea. Even if Captain Bell did not like him, even if he did not wish to be bothered, he would have to do it. It was mandatory. Why, Mrs. Benson—there was an absolute certainty. She would miss him later on at the swimming pool, but little Jimmy, good old little Jimmy, would miss him directly after breakfast when he called for him to take a playful romp around the deck. Wonderful little Jimmy; the finest kid in the whole, wide world. Jimmy was a double certainty; as certain as the sunrise every day.

All at once there passed through his body an intense desire to live. His pulse throbbed with the excitement of the emotion, and his heart beat furiously in his breast. He had never felt so strongly on the subject before; he had just lived with scarcely any thinking about it, imagining vaguely that some day, naturally, he would die. But now he saw clearly that life was precious; that everything else, love, money, fame, was a sham when compared with the simple goodness of just not dying.

Seeing that, he suddenly understood the puzzling illness that had forced him to leave New York. All during the trip he had thought about it vaguely, really being afraid to consider the subject too thoroughly. But now he knew what it was, and somehow he found he had the courage to face it. It was the illness of complete negation. During those four days he had lain listlessly in bed there was one hour, the worst of them all, when he had racked his brain without success to find something he wished to do. First, the physical things: he had not wished to eat, was not thirsty, had no sensual desires, was sated with nicotine and alcohol. He had not wished to take any exercise, and yet certainly had no desire to lounge around or sleep. There was absolutely nothing on the physical side he had wanted during that hour; all his sinews were so inert that it did not matter if they were part of him or not. And the mental side had been just as bad. He strongly had not wanted to see anybody, talk and "have fun"; and yet he had not exactly wished to be alone. The little creative ability that was in Standish—he had written a sonnet in his youth—had been dormant during that hour. And so had his intellect. He had not desired to toy with the intricacies of advanced algebra, for example, and at the same time had shuddered at the thought of facing a hard day's work in the office, with telephones constantly jangling and customers forcing him to make quick decisions. Previously he had always been able to dispel such a mysterious attack by "burying himself in work," but during that hour he was too weary even for that. It had been the same on the spiritual side; he had felt no great curiosity about the hereafter or the past, no wonderment about the creation of the world; no desire to go to church and no desire to stay away. He was the completely jaded man at that hour, trapped in a void of nothingness; and that was why it had been so terrible, that was why he had had to get away.

"Now the exact opposite is true," Standish found himself saying aloud. "I'd give anything for a smoke, a drink—oh, my God, I'm talking to myself!"

But it was true; he thought of the waterlogged cigarettes he had thrown away with his coat—how delightful it would be to smoke one of them. How the nicotine would soothe his bursting lungs. How a shot of hot, burning whisky would tingle in his parched throat! And if he could be lounging now in a soft bed, with two white pillows at his head—Olivia at his side in that lace negligee she wore on certain occasions, the perfume of her body making him languorous! He would work, he would play, with a ferocious zest if he could get out of this. He would be a human dynamo at the office during the day, and the toast of his admiring friends at night for his endless appetite for fun—far into each and every night! And on Sundays he would go to church and pray and be a good and a great man, if God and Captain Bell would rescue him now.

"Captain Bell!" Standish cried. "Captain Bell!"

The utter silence following this, his first hysterical outburst, was the most depressing incident Standish had ever gone through. He fairly wilted with the terror of it; his Adam's apple bulged in his throat as he swallowed hard. How tiny was his shriek on the bottomless sea; God must be holding His sides with laughter. A sense of shame overwhelmed Standish; he trod water furiously and looked around to be sure nobody had heard him. But all he saw was the endless swells of the remorseless sea, and the *Arabella* a pinpoint on the horizon.

Standish's eyes grew hard. He made a grim resolve, as the *Arabella* became a mere dot on his panorama. He would use all the gifts God and breeding had given him to get through this alive; stamina and courage and the sharpest edge of his wit. He would conserve every ounce of his energy, prevent sunstroke, stave off thirst and hunger, keep afloat through hour after endless hour, if necessary, by the exercise of an unflagging spirit. All these things he would do, by God, and live to tell the tale! He wished no pity; the mistake was his and his alone, the clown's error of slipping on a grease spot.

He was ready to suffer for it. But he would live!

And then there happened the worst thing yet; happened so swiftly that Standish was caught off his guard. He realized he was thirsty. What started it he did not know, but he suspected he had begun to get thirsty by thinking that he must not. Soon he began reproaching himself for not having gorged himself on water before he fell overboard. It was no time before he was mulling over the great enigma of nature concerning the disproportion between the ocean's contents and its potability. He recalled that before taking the stroll that ended in his plunge he had drunk one cup of coffee, instead of two, as was his usual custom. In fact, he had been going back to get that second cup when he slipped on the grease spot. The more he thought about the wisdom of not thinking how thirsty he was, the thirstier he got until, in a rage, he shouted: "For God's sake, shut up! You're not thirsty. You're only imagining things. Why, you haven't been in the water two hours yet-"

Another awful silence. The second outburst wearied him: he actually was talking to himself, he, Henry Preston Standish, whose ancestors were both sane and distinguished. Standish started to swim around a bit; a gentle, strainless breast stroke. He swam toward the *Arabella,* naturally, which was receding over the horizon. And the sun was high; much higher than when he had slipped on that grease spot.

Standish grew tense; he could feel his heart pounding

within his breast. Half a mile away a school of porpoises were making gentle play in the water. There were at least a dozen of them, and they zigzagged between air and water with superbly graceful leaps; all in all a wondrous spectacle. It was not fear of the porpoises that frightened Standish; he knew they were harmless (and as for the porpoises, they did not even deign to come near him, caution of the unknown overpowering their sense of curiosity); it was, instead, the comparison that made him see so plainly now how unfit he was for habitation of the sea; almost as unfit as his wrist watch, which had died when it touched the first drop of water. What a stretch of centuries between those porpoises and him, and yet he wished he had their gills and tails. "Osmosis," Standish suddenly thought, which made him relax all at once, for that word had not been in his head since he was a freshman in college nineteen years ago.

The porpoises vanished as quickly as they had appeared, leaving Standish with a melancholy feeling of impending disaster. He turned his eyes again toward the *Arabella.* She was gone.

He could not believe it; she had been there just a moment ago; tiny, true, but there, on the horizon, his one remaining link with the world that he knew. Melancholy gave way to despair as his eyes darted furiously around the horizon. And the next moment despair gave way to tears, salt tears that rolled down his cheeks into the salt sea. For he sighted the *Arabella* again;

unknowingly he had looked into the sun for her, and she was now slightly north of the sun. But all he saw was a blur and a smokestack, and sometimes when the swell of the sea before him reached its apogee he saw nothing. He trod water furiously, trying to raise his body high above sea level, straining his tear-filled eyes to see something he did not wish to see: that smokestack sinking inevitably off the rim of his world.

"How cruel, oh, how cruel!" Standish cried. And at the same moment he realized that his wallet bearing his water-soaked money, the photo of his family, and the old speakeasy cards had become detached somehow from his blue-and-yellow shorts and dropped to the bottom of the sea.

Seven

The sun soared high, stayed for a while at the top of the sky, glaring diabolically upon its desolate world, and then, as if making up its mind to take a closer look, began a leisurely descent. The man in the ocean lay in a trance, lost in the contemplation of his fate.

Around three o'clock—judging from the sun's position—Standish looked at his clammy hands. All the pigment had been drained out of them and they were lifelessly white, the colorless color of impending death. His thirst was awful now, and that horrible moment was always on his mind when he had watched the *Arabella* vanish tantalizingly over the horizon. From then on life had not been the same, and time had blended into the monotone of his existence. The color of the sea was blue, and the blueness seeped into his soul. Of all the ways to die, he thought, drowning was the worst, and he wondered why such a fate had been selected for him. This whole ghastly affair upset all his preconceived notions about justice. He had always believed in the law of retribution; for every good you do a good will be done to you, and the same for everything bad. But Standish had never done anybody any great harm. True, he had lost money for some men when the stock market crashed, but that had not really been his fault. He had been, on the whole, honest, kind, and just, so why were the fates being dishonest, cruel, and so damnably unjust to him? Why not Pym, why not put the grisly finger on Pym, or even Bingley? He realized all at once the awful thing about death by drowning in a calm blue sea—the time on your hands to think and curse your fate, to feel so helplessly small and terrified, to watch the very marrow being sucked out of you.

The only food on which a drowning man could subsist was hope of being rescued; otherwise all sanity must be lost. And yet, though he imagined there was not much hope, he still kept his sanity. In a way, this puzzled him; by all rights he should be raving mad now, driving away his remaining strength in one wild outburst of heartrending hysteria. But he was not mad in the least; he was perfectly sane, and miserably unhappy. Standish decided he was such a well-bred man that he could not go insane. It was not in him to lose a grip on himself;

without great difficulty, he realized, he was taking notes on his own pain, just as he used to watch the stocks rise and fall on the ticker back home.

The sun was dreadfully hot now, and just looking at it, so impossibly fiery and big, and then casting his bloodshot eyes around the incredibly vast and lonely sea, with those pitiless stretches of water, all in a giant circle more precise than anything that could ever be drawn by man, made Standish feel faint and sick.

He tried not to look about him. He tried to keep his eyes shut and, floating on his back in that position he had prized so dearly as a youth, but which was now becoming increasingly agonizing, imagine he was somewhere else. He imagined he was in his office, in Olivia's arms, in the Oranges sitting on a rocking chair and talking to his mother and father, or in Hawaii reclining on an easy chair and gazing at night out to the surf rolling in on Waikiki. But he realized bitterly after a while that this attempt to deceive himself was so childish that it deservedly met with little success. For always there crept into his mind the futile resentment of his destiny, the absolute unfairness of it all. God should be ashamed of Himself, Standish thought, for permitting such a terrible thing. Other men who fell off ships, men much worse than he, men who had never done a good deed in their wasted lives, were treated more kindly. Fishing boats picked them up; the current carried them to shore; pieces of wreckage, priceless rotted lumber, floated in their path, enabling them to rest for a while, to forgo the unendurable strain of lying in one position and keeping their bursting, exhausted lungs forever filled to the brim with air. Other men got all these breaks, but God would not even send Standish a matchstick.

"Why?" Standish cried out. "Why?" And then he realized it was the first time he had spoken since noon, when the sun was directly above him. His voice filled him with incalculable despair, so echoless it was in this watery void. Apparently there was no answer to his question, which was, he realized, purely and excusably rhetorical. There was not, and could never again be, an answer to anything from now on; life was all mixed up; the good people were abused and tortured; villains laughed and lived; and every proverb, including even "you can't eat your cake and have it," an atrocious lie.

The sun was at its hottest now, which meant, he imagined, that the time was around half-past three. But he felt he could not even be sure of that; it would certainly be three-thirty without any question to anybody else, but Standish did not believe in anything any more. However, granting it might be three-thirty, that meant he had been in the water more than ten hours. Ten hours! Great things had happened in ten hours. Henry Preston Standish, Jr., the male who would carry on the good Standish name, was born in less than ten hours, from the first labor pain to the last. Fortunes had been won and lost in less time, and here Standish was in the water ten hours and nothing decisive had happened.

But when Standish thought about it in another light he felt proud of himself. Many men, he knew, would have died within ten hours. Most men would not have had a heart as stout as his in such a situation. The thirst alone, the cruel, insidious thirst, would have killed them off like gnats before a flame. All at once new hope surged in Standish's breast; he would be rescued; he knew he would be rescued. That cook, that idiotic lout of a cook, surely would be missing him by this time. The steward, little Jimmy! The cook was a human being and as such possessed a brain, no matter how inconsequential it was or how poorly it functioned. God would put the thought into his sluggish brain if he could not put it there himself. The *Arabella* would turn around and find him; no doubt she already had done so and any moment would reappear over the horizon, headed straight for the seaspeck that was he. Three more hours yet before darkness; plenty of time, and he would live through it, by all that was holy!

"Oh, God!" Standish cried. "Oh, dear God!

Oh, good, kind God!" His voice was tragically strident, for he saw in a flash the reason for his new optimism. The thought of suicide had crept subtly into his mind; that was it. And that was his way of fighting it, to feign courage in the face of this new threat to his sanity.

From the very first moment he started to think about it he knew he would not commit suicide; the Standishes were not the suicide kind.

And yet, for some sadistic reason he could not fully analyze, he decided to permit himself the pleasure of thinking about it deliberately as he lay there in the water, finding every new breath a decided effort. First of all, no one would ever know about it. That was grimly funny, a noble jest. No little paragraph in the newspaper, no whispering at the club or behind Olivia's back. That, so far as he could see, was the only really advantageous point he had scored since he had slipped like an uncouth backwoods hick on that damned grease spot. It would be impossible to check the facts, granting that some day his body would be found. For all he would have to do would be to let the air out of his lungs, which was not an effort, but a lack of effort, and permit his face to drop a mere two inches from its present position. Why, the water was lapping around his nostrils now; an inch would suffice. Let out your breath and submerge and then, suddenly, with the last ounce of will and energy left in your body, inhale deeply, not of the air, but of the blue water. Then, Standish presumed, there would ensue a desperate struggle; his reflexes probably would discharge the water from his lungs, and he would flail up to the surface, beating his arms, coughing, spitting, and gasping for air. But if he inhaled the water with sufficient determination—all depended on that one mighty underwater breath—the struggle would be a short one. All his pain and fear would be ended, his thirst assuaged; and never again would he have to assume that miserable position of the arched back, the pointed toes, and the outstretched arms. Standish decided to try it—up to the point of inhaling the water—just to see how it would feel.

He let the air out of his lungs and permitted his body to sink pleasantly under the water; as he closed his eyes he was catapulted back to his childhood days when he used to hold his nose and duck his head in the bathtub. It was delightful under the water, just sinking lazily; he knew and even felt sorry the experiment would be over in a few seconds and he would have to rise to the surface for air again. Suddenly he felt an overwhelming temptation to proceed a little further with the experiment; just breathe in a little water and see what would happen. Men had jumped off roofs with less provocation, and any change would be for the best in his present situation.

Standish almost did; but then a remarkable thing happened. He got a feeling of absolute certainty that he would be rescued; he imagined he heard the *Arabella's* vibrations in the water. Automatically he bobbed up to the surface and frantically swallowed the fresh salt air. He scanned the horizon for the *Arabella,* but she was not anywhere in sight. Exhausted, Standish resumed the floating position, feeling strangely awed.

After that, time dissolved into a hazy thought; the pain in his back reached a certain stage of persistent dullness and grew neither better nor worse. The job of keeping afloat, which depended on the speed with which he could discharge the air from his lungs and draw in fresh air, lapsed into a wearisome, unpleasant routine, as if he were working for hours in front of some machine that forced him to do the same simple task, unchanging and unending, thousands of times without rest.

"Olivia...children, Junior, Helen. It was pretty awful, but I got used to it after a while. I don't think I can describe how it feels to be all alone in the middle of the ocean, but I'll try. I am only five feet, seven inches tall, and I weigh one hundred and forty-five pounds. But God alone knows how deep the ocean is, or the total weight of the water. Just think of it, Olivia, Junior, Helen! As far as your eyes can scan, in front of you and in back of you, stretches the water. And above you the sky and the sun. That is your whole world; nothing to break the monotony of the scene. And a speck of something set down in the exact center of the picture. That is me, your husband and your father. Sometimes I thought I wouldn't have strength to stay afloat until they came and picked me up. Pass the cigarettes, please, Olivia. And a match. Thank you. Then lying there on my back" (no, better tell them I was swimming around all the time) "swimming around in that God-forsaken sea, I came face to face with a school of porpoises. We were so close that they could have eaten out of my hand. I wasn't scared. No sense getting scared. Did you ever see a school of porpoises playing at the bow of a ship? Prettiest sight in the world. But

I never thought I'd come face to face with them in the sea. Yes, Olivia, I believe I will have another scotch and soda."

The thought of a scotch and soda was too much. "Man overboard!" Standish shouted in a voice hoarse from thirst. Then he moaned like a fretful child. How much more humane it would have been if he had been mangled by the *Arabella's* propeller and instantly killed. A swift, sharp pain was far superior to a slow, dull one, and sudden death kinder than the endless agony of futile hope.

He suddenly realized his blue-and-yellow shorts and tight-fitting athletic shirt were a heavy weight. In a fitful outburst of temper he started ripping them off his body. The shorts came off easily, but he had to tug and strain hard to pull off the undershirt. He flailed around insanely in the water, tugging madly at the shoulder straps. Finally they came off somehow; he was free and naked. Being naked was a new sensation for which Standish was momentarily grateful. For a while he actually felt comfortable in the water. But then he realized with stark terror that that was because all his life swimming in the nude had been a pleasure, a relaxation, something to look forward to on a hot day. At the Athletic Club in New York, in the strictly male swimming pool that smelled of chlorine, he had swum naked on many pleasant occasions. Now being naked had a far different significance, and it made him shudder and feel clammily cold and exhausted when he thought about it. He had stripped to the flesh to prepare himself for death—it was as simple as that. Undertakers stripped their victims before dressing them for burial. But Standish had to strip himself, while still alive, and there would be no burial for him after he died.

"Think of Olivia!" Standish said aloud.

"Olivia—lying in the water, hour after hour, sometimes I thought of the most horrible things. But I always closed my eyes and saw a picture of you and the children when things looked blackest. And I never actually lost all hope."

Huge tears rolled from Standish's smarting, half-blinded eyes. It was such a magnificent story to tell, if only he could be rescued! The world needed the story: a tale of courage in the face of the most elemental kind of disaster, a tale of hope being nourished by a stout heart.

His voice cried out in a wilderness of water: "Listen to me! Somebody please listen!"

But of course nobody was there to listen, and Standish considered the lack of an audience the meanest trick of all.

Eight

Dinner that evening, served promptly at five aboard the *Arabella,* was a great success. There was, to start with, clam chowder, which was followed by grilled herring, lamb cutlets, roast turkey with chestnut stuffing, Russian and beetroot salads, roast potatoes, cauliflower, apple pie, marrons Chantilly, cheese, fruits, coffee, and tea. The food was not at all extraordinary, the cook being a man of average talents, but it was both wholesome and tasty, and there was plenty of it. No more was needed aboard the *Arabella.* On such a calm sea, with the gorgeous free pageant of the heavens astounding the aesthetic senses, the appetite needed no tonic. To the disappointment of the steward there had not been a single cocktail or scotch and soda order before dinner—not even from Mr. Standish—and he had remarked to the cook in the course of setting the tables that he had never before sailed with such a collection of dull passengers.

Mrs. Benson's children were so hungry that they ate their dinner in comparative peace and set an all-time record for non-squirming. Mr. and Mrs. Brown had never observed to each other that continuous contemplation of the glories of God usually whets the appetite, but they very well could have, for it proved true in their case. Nat Adams had a naturally keen appetite, which was sharpened by the thought that the whole trip had been paid for in advance and every morsel he ate was just so much out of the company's pocket; and anyway he always had liked roast turkey with chestnut stuffing. The officers and engineers were as famished as usual, and did not talk too much during dinner. One by one they rose from the festive boards (except Mr. and Mrs. Brown, who rose together) and ambled out of the saloon and up to the boat deck, each choosing his favorite spot to digest his food and watch the sun go down.

Meanwhile Captain Bell, with Mr. Prisk at his heels, had been angrily searching the ship.

The good captain had been piqued at first; later he grew angry, and when he subsequently discovered Mr. Prisk's news was true and Standish really was missing, his rage knew no bounds. Returning to the privacy of his cabin, he cursed and reviled Mr. Prisk for not having reported his suspicions to him sooner. He threatened him with all sorts of ghastly punishments, said he would take his license away, throw him in irons, and send him to jail when the *Arabella* reached Panama. Mr. Prisk accepted the master's outburst with the greatest of stoicism, understanding it was a tradition of the sea for a skipper to go through these antics in such a situation. Captain Bell never carried out any of his threats, and Mr. Prisk is still working under him, though on a different ship and a different ocean.

Finally, in real high dudgeon, Captain Bell decided to call all hands to the saloon for questioning. Mr. Prisk quit his skipper's company with relief, cursing very silently. Approaching each passenger, officer, and crew member separately, he said softly: "Please go to the saloon. Captain Bell has an announcement to make." Even though he tried to do his work as undramatically as possible, he created a great deal of excitement among the ship's company. Any untoward incident aboard a ship is welcome, and in fifteen minutes they all were gathered in the saloon, merrily buzzing with conversation. Nobody had the slightest inkling why they were gathered there, not even the officers and engineers, which made it all the more mysterious. For a while all sorts of odd rumors flew about, such as there being a deadly pestilence on the *Arabella,* or there having just been received the news of some terrible calamity in the United States, perhaps a destructive earthquake. In all the flurry the absence of Standish was not noted by a single soul. The buzz of their voices increased to a healthy drone, but ceased almost entirely when Captain Bell made his dramatic appearance around six o'clock.

The captain's face was stern, his lips pressed close together, as he strode to a table in a corner where he could address them all. He looked about him imperiously for a long moment before speaking.

"Ladies and gentlemen," said Captain Bell, "Mr. Standish is missing."

The effect caused by his words was strange indeed; there was a sort of concerted gasp, then a concerted silence, and finally an outbreak of voices everywhere. The speed with which they grasped the captain's announcement showed that almost all of them had known Standish was missing for many hours, but had simply refrained from talking about it. For most, it confirmed an inexplicable uneasiness lying hidden deep within them; now that someone had spoken, it astounded all of them that none had brought the matter to light before.

Captain Bell put up his hand. "Please, please." There was quiet. "From what we know so far, the gentleman was last seen around five o'clock this morning. Has any one of you—please think carefully—seen Mr. Standish since that hour?"

There was a deep silence. Captain Bell cleared his throat. "Mr. Brown—I believe you told Mrs. Benson around ten o'clock that you had seen Mr. Standish in the library at about half-past nine."

Mr. Brown's voice was smooth and dignified. "Yes, that is so, Captain, but I was in error. I explained to Mr. Prisk several hours ago that it was Mr. Adams I really saw in the library. I cannot understand how I got the two men confused. My mind was on other matters, I am afraid."

"That's all right; we all make mistakes," Captain Bell said. "But I just want to be sure. Mr. Adams, you were in the library around half-past nine, weren't you?"

Nat Adams was in a daze. "Yes, sir, I stepped in for a few minutes. Five o'clock this morning!

That's thirteen hours——"

"Yes," Captain Bell said gloomily. "Thirteen hours. But please, all of you, think deep down inside. Doesn't anybody remember seeing Mr. Standish after five o'clock?"

Nobody remembered. Almost everybody felt faint and bewildered. Captain Bell realized the futility of questioning them any further; it was apparent the cook was the only one who had seen Standish at five o'clock, and no one had seen him later.

"Thank you," Captain Bell said finally. "We will have to turn around to search for Mr. Standish. The *Arabella* will be at least a day late in Panama."

The captain was in a rage he found it difficult to control before the passengers. He strode out of the saloon and up to the bridge. He ordered the *Arabella* turned around and headed back toward Honolulu. He ordered the third mate to prepare the searchlights on the bridge for use during the night, and he ordered all hands to stand by, though he knew there was really nothing that could be done. It galled him to do all this, but he knew he would have to make a show of searching for at least twelve hours; until morning at any rate. That would mean a whole day lost. It would cost the company at least five hundred dollars, just when they were trying so hard to economize. Before he stalked off the bridge and back to his cabin he ordered the searchlights swung back and forth for a test, though it was still light, and he realized they would do as much good as flicking a paper match into the face of the sun.

In the saloon there was a period of subdued murmuring, interspersed with clicking of tongues, sighs, and light whistling sounds. The officers, engineers, and crew departed to talk about the news in their own quarters, and most of the passengers suddenly found themselves with the desire to be alone. Even Mr. and Mrs. Brown stopped searching out new meanings from an old *Christian Science Monitor,* and separated. The cook felt ashamed and miserable; he walked to the fateful doorway and stood there a long time. After a while he shuddered, seeing some awful symbolism in the fact that he had thrown the poached eggs into the sea after Standish. Little Jimmy Benson's reaction was negligible, considering the depth of his friendship with Standish. He looked out at the sea and tried to think about Standish being in the water, but it was too much for him, and he never missed any sleep or oatmeal over the matter. The steward's first thought was that he would not get his tip, and his second thought was that he was sorry he had not filched the polka-dot cravat.

Mrs. Benson walked in a dream to a spot behind a lifeboat where she could be alone. The sun was going down and the stars were coming out dimly. The way it happened always reminded her of the lights being put on gradually in a movie theater; going to a movie would be the first, maybe the second, thing she would do upon reaching shore. She gazed furtively out at the ocean. She was here, safe on the broad wooden planks, and Mr. Standish was there, in the water. It was hard to imagine and harder to believe; and yet she knew it was so. He had been such a nice, dignified man, too—she took a package of peppermint drops from her pocket and put one ruminatively in her mouth—always having a kind word for the children, forever attentive, and a gentleman in a lady's presence. A chill crept down her spine, a very little chill, but big enough to make her take a step back from the edge of the deck. There had been a mystery about that man; she had sensed it from the beginning. A brooding quality, something sad and intangible, pervaded his being. From the few words he had said to her the few times he was expansive she guessed he was unhappy, though she could not gather why. But such a way to commit suicide, to leap into the ocean without telling a soul, was beyond her comprehension. There were some things a person could imagine, and some a person could not. Mrs. Benson found it impossible to concentrate on a man adrift in the ocean. She bit into the peppermint drop and chewed it until it burned her tongue.

Nat Adams was troubled so much by the whole sad business that he had another glass of lemonade, which was always on tap in the saloon. Not even to leave an explanatory note behind; it was incredible. He drank it slowly, running the sourness around his mouth, and swallowed reluctantly, thinking how different things might have been if he had knocked on Standish's door after breakfast. He might have knocked a second time and a third, and he might very well have discovered Standish's absence in the morning, when there was still an even chance of turning around and finding him. He went down to his favorite spot on the well deck and gazed out at the sea and the materializing stars in the heaven. It defied his imagination. You could not think of this vastness one moment and then the next moment think of a puny bundle of humanity lost in its midst. One was so much bigger than the other; the human mind simply could not cope with the two together. Nat filled his massive old pipe and puffed on it stoically, his face a wizened mask. There was a clue to Standish's suicide; somewhere in the back of his mind he had a clue. He felt he had to find it. Nat spit into the sea. It came to him all at once; something Standish had said in the course of an idle conversation almost a week ago.

"A pity a man can't live like this forever, just feeling happy without having to think for a reason," Standish had said slowly, gazing at the setting sun. That was the clue. Nat tamped his pipe and hurried back to the saloon; he had to tell somebody about that; maybe they would have statements from Standish in return which, pieced together, would form the pattern of the crazy-quilt.

In the forecastle Bjorgstrom, the Finnish sailor, was feeling both mellow and miserable; even more so than his good friend Gaskin, who was standing by on the bridge, ready to work one of the searchlights. Bjorgstrom had good eyes; he had sharper eyes than any sailor alive, though he did not boast about it. If there were any hope of finding Standish, Bjorgstrom would have stood on the forecastle head in a tropical hurricane, those eyes piercing around the ocean. He would have permitted them to tie him to the mast—if there were any hope. But Bjorgstrom thought there wasn't any hope; his sailor's judgment told him Standish was missing too many hours to be found, except by a miracle. There was not time alone against the man; there was the current always moving him off the *Arabella's* trail. Bjorgstrom sighed and got off his bunk and went up to the poop deck. He stood there in a pair of dirty dungarees, watching the foaming wake of the *Arabella* dissolve into the night. Standish was a good man; Bjorgstrom had spotted him right off as a good man. Bjorgstrom was funny that way; he would appraise passengers the first day out and never change his opinion of them, though it really did not matter, because their paths never crossed. He had appraised Standish immediately as a good man; that is to say, a man who was kind to his mother and sent his money home for his children. Bjorgstrom spent several idle minutes wondering how Standish had lost the money that forced him to commit suicide. Probably in the stock market, he decided vaguely. That was the way it always happened; you are rich, suddenly you lose all your money in the stock market, probably on account of that amazing rogue Ivar Kreuger, and then people get after you to arrest you. In disgrace you flee your family, but finally you learn the police are about to catch up with you, so you kill yourself. It was amazing how consistent was the pattern of the lives of gentlemen such as Standish. Himself, he would never die that way. It was impossible to put into words, but he had a respect for the sea; he took his cap off before it. The sea was a strange person with all sorts of strange ideas even worse than himself when he got drunk. Sailors sail on the sea and the sea says all right, but don't push. Take it easy; you go your way and let me go mine. Once Bjorgstrom had sailed on an American passenger liner plying between New York and Havana, but he quit after one voyage, even though he needed the job badly. Those frivolous people with their cocktails and their dancing in the moonlight, they had no respect at all for the sea. They thought God made the sea to entertain them, while every sensible sailor knew God made it to transport merchandise quietly from one continent to another. As a result the sea got angry and reminded them of their arrogance every once in a while, burning them in a fire aboard ship, freezing them in a northwester, or beating their brains out against mile-high waves. And it was so funny how easily the sea put them in their places, easier than an elephant stepping on an ant. That was why, Bjorgstrom thought hazily, sailors did not wash more than they had to. Landlubbers who did not understand the sea imagined it was because sailors were naturally dirty, but it was only because they did not wish to get too much of the sea on them. The sea got on them enough as it was; spray was always blowing into their faces and in stormy weather waves mounted the well deck. The sea was on all sides of them except up, and God was just as undependable; you never knew what He was going to do either. If the sea so desired, it could give you a bath right this minute—a long bath—so what was the sense in pressing the issue? Poor man, Bjorgstrom thought. But after all it was Standish's own business if he wished to commit suicide. As for himself, he would return to the forecastle and try to write a letter to his mother in Finland.

Nat Adams went into the saloon, his false teeth hurting him, as was always the case when he got excited, and found Mrs. Benson, Mr. Travis, the chief engineer, and Mr. and Mrs. Brown sitting there amidst an air of respectful gloom. Mr. Travis had done all he could, which amounted to turning the *Arabella* around. An absorbing interest in machinery and the eternal necessity of keeping everything oiled had coated his soul with cynicism about human affairs, and he found the absence of Standish did not affect him one way or another. But somehow he felt it befitted his position to show a little concern; so reluctantly he gave up his bridge game for the remainder of the evening and decided to sit in sorrow with the passengers until they made up their minds to go to bed.

Mr. and Mrs. Brown were in a dilemma over more matters than one. The mistake about the man in the library—even Mr. and Mrs. Brown had stopped thinking about it to themselves as a downright lie—had left a bad taste in their mouths, though they did not admit it to each other. Mrs. Brown knew her husband had lied; they were so close together that he could not put anything over on her. But with the same logic they were so close that the lie was hers as much as his; at any rate it had been spoken for her good as well as Mr. Brown's. The general effect of the mistake had been to give Mr. Brown more prominence in the case of Mr. Standish than anyone aboard the *Arabella* with the exception of the cook. Mr. Brown had been constrained to say several times to various persons: "I could have taken an oath it was Mr. Standish, but later, on sober reflection, I realized how greatly I had erred. The eye is indeed deceptive when the mind is taken up with other matters." Not that anyone suspected Mr. Brown had lied; there was just the unpleasantness of having to regulate the tongue over a matter that ought to be the subject for unbridled conversation; and, of course, there was a twinge of conscience, for he could not help thinking that, if he had not uttered the lie, Mrs. Benson might have gone looking for Standish and discovered his absence. However, that was quite far-fetched, and Mr. Brown did not exactly reach the point of reproaching himself and calling himself a cold-blooded murderer. There was another matter that was even more of a dilemma. They had no way of knowing whether Standish was dead or alive; the only thing they could be sure of was that he had attempted suicide. If he was still alive, in spite of his attempt at suicide, they could pray for his rescue and salvation. But if he was dead, which seemed likely, he had taken his own life, which could not be morally countenanced under any circumstance. A sinner who could be saved was all right, but a sinner who was beyond salvation because of death resulting from his sin was about the lowest form of religious fodder Mr. Brown could imagine. Mr. Brown knew the others were expecting him to offer up a prayer; in fact, he knew from long experience among the heathen Chinese that they dreaded it; but the baffling problem perplexed him so greatly that his tongue was tied.

It was such a company that Nat Adams joined. He sat down, burrowing his back comfortably into an easy chair. They greeted him only with sober nods and respectfully lowered eyes, and continued the silence that had existed before his arrival. But Nat was not to be daunted by the silence; his discovery was too much on his mind.

"Ah, poor man," said Nat. "I never thought he'd be the one to go like that."

Mrs. Benson stirred in her chair. All of them had been over this ground many times already. "It makes me sick to think about it, Mr. Adams." Nat gazed solemnly and doggedly at Mr. and Mrs. Brown and Mr. Travis.

"I wonder why he did it," Nat said.

Mr. Brown's voice was sharp. "Apparently some secret sorrow was too powerful for his soul to cope with." He did not approve of this turn of the conversation; the others could see it in the sudden sternness of his wife's face.

But Nat persisted. He crossed his legs, moved forward in his easy chair, and said dreamily: "Strange, Mrs. Benson, but I just realized Mr. Standish was thinking about it all the time, while we thought he was happy. Only a week ago he said to me: 'Adams,' he said, 'a pity a man can't live like this forever, just feeling happy without having to think for a reason.'" Mrs. Benson's eyes were watery. "There was a sadness about him; such a nice sadness. But I never thought it was serious."

"Men are mysterious sometimes," Mr. Travis said, feeling he ought to say something.

Nat put his hand to his chin. "I wonder what he meant by that. I wonder—was he a married man?"

"He was," Mrs. Benson said. "Of course he was. Didn't he ever tell you about his two children back in New York?"

Nat put up his hand. "I don't mean that. He mentioned the kids to me. I mean—was he married now? Seems to me he looked like a man who might have had some trouble with his missus." Mrs. Benson's eyes grew suddenly bright. "Yes, Mr. Adams, yes! Of course. How blind I was not to see it! A few days ago, last Sunday after dinner, I was telling him about Mr. Benson and myself, how well we get along, don't you know; and do you know what he said to me? He looked at me in a funny, unhappy way and said: 'Yes, Mrs. Benson, it makes things easier to be happily married, doesn't it?'" A silence followed her words and she hastened to explain: "It was the way he said it! There was something hidden in his voice; he was envying me, only in a nice way."

"He was always writing letters to her," Mr. Travis said. "I helped the skipper lock up his trunk and personal effects just a while back. There was a letter to her on the desk. It was sealed," he added hastily. "She lives on Central Park West. That's a pretty swell neighborhood. Kept women and all that kind of stuff, so they say," he concluded lamely, finding Mrs. Brown suddenly gazing his way.

Nat shook his head back and forth sadly. "I wonder how she'll feel when she finds out."

"No woman is worth that much," Mr. Travis said, and was sorry the next moment. "Present company excepted." But nobody laughed.

Mrs. Benson found the words flying swiftly from her mouth: "You're perfectly right. No woman is worth dying for. But I'm not one to defend my sex; there are good women and there are bad ones. She must have treated him pretty terribly to drive him to suicide. I bet I can tell you just the kind of woman Mrs. Standish is: a woman cold as ice, without a heart. Probably flirted with every Tom, Dick, and Harry, and finally ran off with another man."

"But even so," Nat broke in excitedly, "would I or any other man in this room jump off a boat in the middle of the ocean on account of a woman?"

"There were children," Mrs. Benson said. "And Mr. Standish was the quiet, home-loving kind; you could see that easily. He seemed so lost traveling around. He must have felt his life was broken up when his wife ran off with that gigolo; he must have taken this trip to try to forget it all; but I guess he just couldn't forget."

Nat's eyes were sad. "There was always a kind of gaunt look about him; like he was hungry-"

"He was miserable," Mrs. Benson said. "He was eating his heart out. Poor Mr. Standish!" Night was falling quickly now; soon the searchlights would be flitting over the sea. The *Arabella* sighed through the cerulean blue, as if her bones were reluctant to turn back after coming so far in one direction. Captain Bell paced the green carpet in his cabin, spluttering indignantly to himself. In the forecastle the men lay quietly, a sullen anger in their eyes, as if they were reproaching the missing Mr. Standish for spoiling the even tenor of their voyage. The radio operator already had sent a brief message to the company's office in Panama, advising them of the catastrophe; but Captain Bell had thought it wise to send no message to Mrs. Standish until he was certain her husband was beyond rescue. He was certain already, but he wished to be certain beyond the shadow of a doubt; a fine fool it would make of him if he sent the message and then, by some accident, they picked up the man.

The third assistant engineer, a young, happy-go-lucky fellow, strolled into the saloon and said to the steward: "Scotch and soda." Then he turned to Mr. Travis. "Bugsy just made a grand slam!"

"Bugsy did!" Mr. Travis got up and, his eyes shining with incredulity, unceremoniously left the company, also leaving them in ignorance of the identity of Bugsy.

Old Nat sat there reflectively, trying to think of Standish, but against his will funny little thoughts crept into his mind: things he had said to his wife before she died many years ago, the time he had fallen off a hay wagon when in his teens. Mrs. Benson was sighing peacefully and pleasantly, and Mr. and Mrs. Brown were lost in a world of religious abstractions.

"Well," Mrs. Benson said out of the blue, "at least he died a quick death."

Mr. and Mrs. Brown started moving their lips simultaneously in prayer, but no one ever discovered whether they were praying for Mrs. Benson or Mr. Standish. The third assistant engineer put a record on the phonograph and soon a trio of girls were harmonizing an innocent little tune, something about frustrated love.

Mr. and Mrs. Brown rose abruptly and at the same time.

"Let us take a stroll around the deck and look at the stars," said Mr. Brown to Mrs. Brown. "Yes," said Mrs. Brown, "let us."

Nine

"I was lying in the sea and my back hurt and my tongue stuck to the roof of my mouth."

Standish was thinking of the day when he would reach Panama aboard the *Arabella* and the reporters would flock around him to inquire how it felt to be stranded in the sea so long. There would be so many of them that he would suggest they go into the saloon.

"Let us go into the saloon and be comfortable," Standish mumbled.

"Let us."

Then Standish tried to recall the name of that society girl who tripped down a flight of stairs on the night of her debut. He racked his brain, but never quite reached the point where he remembered her name, which was (and still is) Miss Adelaide Van Devander. He thought about this and other things at random, because he realized the sun was going down. Now that was a funny thing indeed; when the sun was high in the heavens it seemed hours before it moved an inch across the sky, but once it neared the horizon it plunged with terrible swiftness toward the fatal line.

It would grow dark when the sun crossed that line. Every breath he took was an impossible task; and all his muscles were strained beyond human endurance. All at once Standish realized something tragic: people do not really think about death until it is right on top of them. Several times in the last few hours he had composed himself, in a manner of speaking, and cast his mind reverently on the subject of the hereafter. But the only result had been that his mind played ghastly tricks on him, always twisting his thoughts around until he was dwelling again on the possibility of being rescued. But now he felt a subtle change taking place in his brain. Standish decided this change had its roots in the inevitable accident that had occurred ten minutes ago. Keeping afloat had become a reflex action for him; he had breathed in and out monotonously and automatically at the right times, always managing to keep his nose above water by the merest fraction of an inch. But ten minutes ago exhaustion had forced a slip-up. He had permitted his nose to sink under the water and had started to take a breath without thinking. He had inhaled a lot of water and for a few fear-stricken moments had coughed and spit out his terror into the sea. Exhausted, he had lain back on the water again, but that was the beginning of the subtle change, which enabled him, he saw now, to think a bit more consistently about death.

Through half-blinded eyes Standish watched the sunset. The sun seemed to say: "I will put on a show for you such as you have seldom seen." The sun seemed to puff out its chest and boast about its splendor, declaiming: "Watch me streak this purple around the sky. Here's a streak of delicate pink a thousand miles long. And here's a blend of color man has no word for, except to say it is lovely."

Standish realized the swell of the sea was growing slightly stronger. He felt an awful chill creeping over his numbed blue body. Well, Olivia would have enough insurance and an interest in the firm of Pym, Bingley, and Standish—or perhaps it would revert to Pym and Bingley after a conventional period of mourning. He rather suspected it would, but realized there was nothing he could do about it. The children were rather young to be without a father, but Standish imagined Olivia would remarry after a while. She was beautiful and still youthful-looking, and he did not hold the thought against her, because he had had her first. However, there would be the bother of giving up the apartment on Central Park West owing to his death, a custom he always had believed was senseless. Worst of all, there would be the week or maybe month of unhappiness for Olivia after she learned of his demise. It galled Standish to think that Olivia must be made unhappy on account of a grease spot.

But he suddenly thought that at least this was a clean way to die; your body was washed thoroughly, and no clammy undertaker's hands on it, either. It was a hard way to die, but at least there was none of this useless lingering in an expensive hospital room under an oxygen tent. It really was a dignified way to die, though cruel to those who loved you, because the circumstances spoiled their chance to shed tears at the proper moment; they really would have to cry spasmodically, not knowing whether the tears were doing any good to their own souls. It was a lonely way to die, but that made no difference, for all deaths, including the few seconds of falling off a roof, were singularly and completely lonely; a man thought only about himself at the very end. It was a noble way to die, too, because of its extreme loneliness. Few men since time began had died in exactly this way, all by themselves. At sea on a ship the ship became the center of your universe; at sea on your own body you yourself became the knot where all mundane skeins were joined.

For the first time he was able to think clearly about the unfortunate manner in which he had fallen off the *Arabella.* For hours on end, lying in the water, he had berated himself for what he considered was gross stupidity. He felt he never would be able to forgive himself for failing to attract the attention of his shipmates directly after he fell overboard. But now he understood how inexorable was nature's attitude toward all life. A little more lung power, he thought, and he would have been safe aboard the *Arabella* at this moment, probably digesting his dinner and talking to Nat Adams. But that was nature's way; she gave you certain characteristics with which to fight your battles in the world, and it was sink or swim with what she handed out. Some men had brawn, others brain; some speed, others stamina. Yokels and opera singers had strong, husky voices, but they were no good in a brokerage office. No matter what you had, you had to be content with it; that was the point. You could not send yourself back to the gods and get another package. And Standish knew now what he possessed. Culture of a sort, including ingrained mannerisms of gentility and a mind that appreciated the quieter, "finer" things in life. Also a code that was iron-bound: be kind to children, bow to ladies though not too sweepingly, walk on the right side of the street, and all that sort of rot. Not much good, really no good at all, for ocean swimming, Standish realized; except that part of the code that gave him what was known as an iron will.

When he looked at things in this light he felt much better, despite his pain and torturing thirst. The sun was now an orange ball of fire speeding to a rendezvous in the part of the world beneath the horizon. The panic grabbed Standish by his shoulders when he looked at the sun. You could look at the sun now for minutes on end without having to lower your eyes. Standish realized that his eyes, now almost completely blind, saw only the sun setting on the remorseless sea.

"Thirteen hours adrift," Standish muttered. "They surely know I'm missing by this time, don't they? That's reasonable, isn't it? They must have turned around to look for me at least five hours ago. The ship has searchlights. They can find me at night. I must help them find me!"

Imperceptibly, day was fading, and though he could hardly see he could sense the subtly changing colors of the ocean and sky. Mrs. Benson was on her way to Panama to meet Mr. Benson; Nat Adams was going to take a pleasant jaunt through Central America. Standish felt he must reach Olivia if only to see her and talk to her for a moment. Suddenly he felt his heart beating wildly, and then aching terribly inside his breast. It had never acted that way before; always it had been a good heart, a true heart, keeping well in the background of his life, doing its work quietly and thoroughly. And now the day was ending; night was falling; and his heart was protesting an unendurable burden.

Standish smiled slyly. He would fool them all, whoever they were who were responsible for this. He would swim back to the *Arabella.* He would swim back if he had to swim all night, under the frightening canopy of stars.

He would become the superman of the ages; the reporters would swamp him in Panama and New York and wherever else he went. "The Man Who Swam All Night in a Barren Sea," the headlines would read. He would be awarded medals for bravery, endurance, courage, and hope that never died. Famous athletes would tender him dinners; he would tour the country in triumph. Pym and Bingley both would be thrust into the background by this magnificent feat, and they would have to accept their inferior position gracefully. His children would grow up to be proud of their father, especially Junior, who as a man would understand.

"Count!" Standish cried, though hardly a sound came from his parched throat. "Count and swim. Count and swim."

He started out, after crazily taking his bearings, in the direction of the *Arabella.* It was a great relief to abandon the floating position; and immediately his back felt so much better that he wondered why he had not thought of this before. *"One, two, three, breathe! One, two, three, breathe!"* Henry Preston Standish went plowing through the water, performing a crawl stroke whose excellent form would have gladdened the heart of the swimming coach at the Athletic Club in New York. At times he felt he was a fish destined from the cradle for a life solely in the sea, so smoothly, so neatly, did he progress through the brine. His body responded to the task before it with co-ordination that amazed and gladdened his mind. His toes were pointed, his knees stiff, his hands cupped, and his back arched. As he kicked and beat his arms like a windmill, he breathed out slowly through his nose on three strokes and twisted his head and breathed in quickly through his mouth on the fourth. And in his mind was an overwhelming pride of his uncanny physical powers. With such a heart and such strong muscles, with such indomitable lungs, he would reach the *Arabella* if it took until morning! As he turned his head to breathe while plowing through the water, he could see ahead of him the sun going down on the horizon; now it was spheroid, now a semicircle, now a crescent of orange hue. He felt if he could reach out his hands he could touch it, grasp it, climb up on it and rest his incredibly weary body on its broad rim. The sea was in shadows, and all Standish knew was his pain-racked body speeding through the brine and the sinking ball of orange before his face.

All at once he stopped his frantic swimming; stopped suddenly as if he had hit his head against a brick wall rising out of the sea. It was night; the sun had gone down; there was only its faint aurora on the waters and majestic clouds all above him resplendent in the prismatic colors. And as he stopped, his exhausted body sprawling in the sea, the thought smote him with hideous dismay. He had been swimming the wrong way. With his last strength he had been speeding away from the *Arabella* instead of toward her. He had been swimming into the face of the sun, and the sun set in the west; the sun always set in the west. But the *Arabella* was sailing east, as it had been sailing at sunrise when he fell overboard; east into the sun that would rise the next morning. "Why did I do it?" Standish cried, though no words came from his parched throat. He knew why; the sun was all that had been left for his hope to fasten on; he had forgotten the world had moved on during the thirteen hours he had been in the sea. Now even if the *Arabella* had turned to search for him he had made it more difficult. And he had no strength to start swimming back. And it was evening and would soon be night. It was night already; the dim stars were out, the evening stars, and a blue shadow crept over this dismal world. Through smarting eyes almost completely blind Standish watched the stars come out and write their names on his aching heart. His body shook with agonizing chills. His lips were as purple as the deepening sky, the majestic, breathtaking, and lonely sky. And he knew now there was nothing quite so horrible as being the last man in a flat world, alone in the precise center of a maddening circle. It was too utterly lonely here for a civilized man to bear. Standish began to die. He felt himself dying, and he thought he was glad. Wildly he cast his blind eyes around the dark waters, groping for a bit of wreckage to grasp. But that was only a last defiant gesture from the Standish who wanted to live; the dying Standish had other things to do. Happily and insanely he did something he had been wanting desperately to do for many hours. He submerged and opened his mouth and swallowed impatiently and fully of the bitter salt water. He drank in huge sucking swallows, hardly feeling the water's bitterness, until he knew there was as much water inside him as he could hold; water inside and out and only a collection of bones, blood, and flesh in between.

The next minute Standish was frightfully, pitifully sorry. The relief of drinking was ephemeral; soon he retched and choked in extreme misery. Suddenly he heard himself croaking in an inhumanly hoarse voice: "Help me! Help me!" And then the first cramp seized him. He doubled up like an opera hat with irresistible speed that amazed the tiny segment of his mind still able to observe with some degree of objectivity what was happening. He doubled up, and found to his utter astonishment he was unable to straighten out. Now he was under the water, fighting, kicking, trying to raise two clawing hands to the heavens while he painfully held his breath. The realization that never again would he straighten out—that he would die in a knot—struck him forcibly. The thought hit him as though a fighter had sent a bare-knuckled fist crashing into his jaw. Before he knew what he was doing he had breathed in of the harsh salt water. It burned the inside of his throat as he tried with all the power remaining in his exhausted body to eject it. But when he realized he was trapped, unable to rise to the surface and doomed to suffocate, Standish suddenly stopped struggling. A dismal futility swept through his mind as if a hand of steel that would never relax its grip had seized him by the throat. His face became a mask of utter despair as in a flash he saw and understood the whole ironic story of his misfortune.

They were the Fates; not one Fate, for he could have fought one, but several, and they had swept their eagle's eyes around the world and finally fixed their stares on him: him alone out of all the teeming millions. From that moment on he was just an insignificant mouse which the Fates had shoved around with strong cat's-paws solely for a selfish interlude of sport; shifting him across a continent, sending him through the Panama Canal to San Francisco and up to Alaska and back, forcing him to make a long-distance telephone call to Olivia in New York, shipping him to Honolulu, and sending him down for dinner at the hotel just when that strange man—that man whose face Standish could not remember though he saw everything else with startling clarity—was listening to the desk clerk talking about the *Arabella.* How funny this must have been to the cunning cats that were the Fates; and how hilariously funny now, watching him going through the inescapable death struggle! How they all must be standing around now, bending over and watching, whispering: "Look, see how his face is curling up and his eyes popping out of his head. Don't miss this; this is good. Ha! He's trying to rise to the surface; let's turn on just a little more muscle cramps." How proud they must be of themselves for this magnificent jest: forcing him aboard the *Arabella,* making him like to rise early to see the sunrise, waiting for the thirteenth day and then putting a grease spot under his foot and shoving him overboard with invisible hands. A puppet he was—dangling grotesquely on a stage that was the Pacific Ocean, on strings reaching up to the heavens, all for their morbid amusement.

Standish felt himself strangling; tragically he knew he was dying of suffocation, but somehow he did not want to do anything about it; did not care to struggle any more. The battle was lost; what was the use? But he would show them. He would compose himself and die with dignity; they would not have another chance to laugh at him. He would untangle the lines of pain from his face and then he would die so bravely that a silence would fall upon the whole world. And in the midst of that silence the Fates would stand abjectly, feeling the shame seared upon their backs. The wiseacre smiles would fade from their faces and the remorse would pierce them to the bone, and they never would be able to shake themselves free of it. As a matter of fact, Standish thought, it was awfully quiet now; he had never in all his life remembered it being so completely, so deathly quiet. A sudden unbelievably sharp and overpowering pain crashed down upon his body, as though some fiend had stuck a knife into his neck and slit his throat savagely from ear to ear. That, Standish thought with strange detachment, must be his heart breaking up.

Ten

Not dead yet, Standish thought. And not alive either; before walking away and leaving his inert remains to shift for themselves it would be best to think of life as he had lived it; not of the ordinary events (spanked by his father, coming home one day with his nose bleeding, the girl in that French hotel, almost cornering the market in green peppers) but of the extraordinary things that had happened in his insufficient thirty-five years. And with each thought a pang came to his heart that had shattered, a pang of regret that he could not go on like other men having new extraordinary experiences day after day.

Most extraordinary was that his heart had gone on beating thirty-five years without once stopping to complain about the thankless, endless task. Never in all that time had it occurred to him how important an organism was his heart; never once had he stopped to think that, had his heart desired, it could have killed him long ago merely by deciding to stop beating for half an hour or so.

And extraordinary, too, was that never once before in his whole life had he gone hungry or thirsty. As a youth he had interpreted thirst in terms of ice cream sodas, and later in life when he remarked he was thirsty he meant he would like a beer or scotch and soda. But the real meaning of hunger and thirst, to be hungry for bread and thirsty for water, had not existed for him. Strange that he should be learning so much about life at a time when he did not really know whether he was living or dead. But it had been the same with cigarettes, with nicotine; never in all his seventeen years of smoking had he got the desire for a cigarette without satisfying it. It was indeed extraordinary, when he thought about it, that his whole life had been like that, always getting everything he wanted, and not wanting too much. Sports equipment, bicycles and roller skates when a child; good clothes, foreign travel, and his own car in his teens; money to spend in college, the right clubs; a good business and a good wife and children later on.

He had got all those things, but the one thing he wanted now with a full desire was being denied him. "I got everything without really asking for it," Standish said to himself, feeling strangely cold and numb under the water, "and now I want not to die, but I am not going to get *that.* I know I am not going to get it. No matter how hard I wish, no matter what I do, there is one desire that will not be satisfied."

The thought made him rueful, and in his mind he pursed his lips in a child's pout. Never again would he go walking in Central Park with the children on a Sunday afternoon, passing other fathers, wearing a boutonniere. It struck him as incredible that the world could go on without Henry Preston Standish living on it, and yet he had a strong suspicion that that was exactly what the world intended to do. Yet the world would be remarkably barren with himself under it instead of on it. There would be so many empty gaps impossible to fill that Standish wondered how the world would manage. Who would sit in the easy chair in his library, reading magazines almost every night? That was only one problem. Somebody had to sit in the easy chair; it just could not go on forever without an occupant, because easy chairs were made for people to sit in. Olivia would not be brave enough to sit in it; it would bring back too many memories. And she certainly would not permit another man to sit in it; that would be brazen and not at all in character with Olivia. There would be voids everywhere through no fault of his. A void in the elevator boy's pocket next Christmas, a void in the telephone book, a void on the office stationery. They would even make more voids where they did not have to; they would pay a man to scrape the name of Standish off the door of the firm; the superintendent would remove his name from the letter box. To hundreds of department stores and companies putting out mailing lists the word would soon go around: "Don't send circulars to Henry Preston Standish any more; he's dead."

Standish shook his head wistfully without really shaking it at all. There were so many places where he used to go, where it was natural for him to go, that would contain mere emptinesses from now on. New York City would be dotted with spaces that could never be filled by anyone but the real Henry Preston Standish; his locker at the Athletic Club, the hollow in his bed, the interior of his dinner jacket, to mention just a few. Only the real Standish could fill these spaces; those who came to take his place would be branded as counterfeits by his mother and father, his wife and his children.

Olivia and Junior and Helen—how would they possibly manage to get along without him? You could temporize on the question when you were not really dying, but in your last moments you saw how serious it really was. He had loved Olivia and begotten the children, and they were aware of his part in their lives. Tearing them asunder was like severing Siamese twins; both always died, though the doctors were usually hopeful one would live. Standish acknowledged to himself that husbands and fathers had died before without seriously affecting the lives of their wives and children, but the next moment he decided rather sternly that he was different. Olivia and the children would kill themselves when they learned of his death. It was better that way; better for them all to die at once. Then he would not feel so damnably lonely in the few short steps he must take to his watery grave.

Standish remarked to himself that he felt like the tolling of a bell. This was the first completely irrational remark he ever remembered making, and yet he did not feel foolish about it, for that was exactly how he felt, just like the tolling of a bell. He imagined that if he had been dying in a hospital, with his family gathered around his bed, he never would have thought of such a fantastic thing. But he was far under the ocean, in total blackness, and not breathing any longer; he was full of water, inside and out, and feeling strangely at peace, as though time were standing still. And that first fantastic thought started others crowding into his brain; it was something like a soft nightmare, neither pleasant nor unpleasant, which he once had experienced in New York when he smoked too many cigarettes before going to bed. All his friends, their faces funnily contorted, appeared, stayed a minute to stick out their tongues, and vanished as others pushed their way into the picture, grimacing, puffing out their cheeks and making monsters with their eyes and lips. But they could not deceive him; he could recognize them all. "Come, come," Standish thought, wagging an imaginary finger. "I know who you are; I'm no fool. Stop making faces, Junior! Take off that mask, Helen! Olivia—what in God's name has come over you?"

He thought of his mother, father, and sisters and how he would never talk to them again. He thought of the *Arabella,* how Nat Adams looked without his teeth, and how Mrs. Benson's breasts bobbed in the red bathing suit. Red: Standish could see the color easily, and he decided that in a manner of speaking he loved Mrs. Benson; if it could be arranged he would like to sleep with her. But he saw the difficulties; every once in a while he forgot he was a doomed man and it was damned annoying when he had to remind himself. He decided he would like to sleep with every woman except, possibly, the wives of Pym and Bingley, and maybe set an all-time record for lechery before he went through the final motions of dying. There were no women around, of course, but there might be mermaids. Mermaids! Standish laughed without really laughing. Everybody knew there were no such things as mermaids, but now he was not so sure. There could very well be mermaids; there could very well be a Father Neptune rising out of the ocean bottom and poking the numbness out of Standish with his scepter.

Standish felt himself strangling. The dark world suddenly burst wide in a grandiose display of pyrotechnics. Rockets of brilliant yellow and green exploded before his astonished closed eyes, splattering his firmament with lines and dots and beads of vivid colors. "This is the end," Standish thought, watching the red, the orange, the indigo, and the violet hissing rockets. "They are putting on this display as a send-off for me. It is beautiful; it is astounding; it is also very lonely." Olivia and the children ought to be here to see it; he would hold their hands as the rockets burst and together they would laugh wildly, crazily. "Olivia and the evening star," Standish murmured. "Two children against a cooling sun." And he wondered what he was saying, what meant the garbled words swirling through his brain. "Lonesome...lonesome! Nobody to say good-by to. All by myself, watching myself die..."

(In a quiet section of Westchester, Bingley moved restlessly in his bed, dreaming about a stock market that crashed unremittingly, carrying his fortune away in a flood of crumpled dollars. And who was that man with the death-mask for a face, widening the flood? The clerk in the hotel at Waikiki stopped his writing on a scratch-pad and gazed for a long moment at the surf rolling in upon the narrow beach. Those fools on their surfboards were trying to ride in like Roman conquerors, but most of them fell ingloriously. Not safe, he thought, not safe at all; some day somebody would get hurt. And how was that man getting on, that man he had shipped aboard the *Arabella?* What was his name, anyway, and why think about him at all? In New York Olivia awoke out of a maddening dream; it was half-past one in the morning and she sat bolt upright in bed, trying to remember what she had dreamed; something about a bottomless cavern all completely dark. But she only heard little Helen sobbing in the next room and went inside to comfort her. Junior was silent, lying in his bed, his eyes staring in the darkness. "Mother," he said, "make Helen stop crying." And there was a new tone of authority in the child's voice. Aboard the *Arabella* Mr. Prisk stood on the bridge and watched a meteor streak across the sky and thought how weak were the searchlights Gaskin and another sailor moved slowly across the water. Captain Bell, in his cabin, felt his rage suddenly subside; inexplicably he felt ashamed of himself. He looked at his four-masted schooner, but found no beauty in it. Mr. Prisk was a good first mate; he would not be so gruff with him in the future, though, dammit, you had to keep these fellows in their place. Little Jimmy Benson tossed restlessly in his bunk and unaccountably opened his eyes in the semi-darkness to find his mother was not there; she was pacing the boat deck alone, looking at the stars and wanting desperately to be made love to. Six more days to Panama; she could wait. Old Nat Adams suddenly became aware that the clump of his shoes on the well deck made a dismal, almost echoless sound. "I must get rubber heels like Mr. Standish," he told himself.)

Standish thought that no pain ever again could equal the pain when his heart broke. Out of the deepening purple the words came crazily melodious, sweeping him back into his mother's arms: "You were only hair dust and warm body, a heart beating naked before me and a sorrowful voice like the murmur of water fore-doomed forever to fall from a cave to a cave...."

Herbert Clyde Lewis and the Rescue of *Gentleman Overboard*

by Brad Bigelow

'Listen to me! Somebody please listen!' cries Henry Preston Standish, the hero of Herbert Clyde Lewis's *Gentleman Overboard* as he struggles to stay afloat in the middle of the Pacific Ocean, exhausted and past hope of rescue. 'But of course nobody was there to listen,' Lewis wrote, 'and Standish considered the lack of an audience the meanest trick of all.' Lewis died of a heart attack at the age of 41, broke, out of work and alone in the middle of New York City, a victim of Hollywood blacklisting, his three novels long out of print: a writer who'd lost his audience. No one came to rescue him.

As long as a writer's words are preserved, though, there is a chance of his work being rescued. In the case of *Gentleman Overboard*, it took over seventy years for someone to spot the novel, lost in the ocean of forgotten books. And the rescuers came from around the world: from Argentina, Israel, the Netherlands, and now, England and the United States. Lewis's story of one man dying alone and forgotten is now being discovered by readers who find this slim, sad comedy speaks to a sense of shared loneliness — a sense made universal through the lockdowns and enforced isolation of the COVID-19 pandemic.

Born in Brooklyn in 1909, Lewis was the second son of Jewish immigrants from Russia. His mother Clara came to the U.S. with her family in 1887 at the age of two. His father Hyman arrived a year later at the age of thirteen, apprenticed to work for his older brother Samuel as a tailor. By the time Herbert was born, the Lewises were living in the Brownsville neighborhood around Tompkins and Lafayette Avenues. The area was then the heart of the largest Jewish community outside Europe, the first stop for tens of thousands like Lewis's parents, immigrants from Russia and Eastern Europe. Between 1890 and 1915, the number of Jews living in New York City jumped from under 100,000 to nearly one million. To ease their sons' integration into American life, Hyman changed his family's name from Luria to Lewis and gave them solidly Anglo-Saxon names: Alfred Joseph, Herbert Clyde and Benjamin George.

To Herbert Clyde Lewis, Brownsville was the quintessential American melting pot — at least in hindsight.

In 1943, he wrote an article titled 'Back Home' for The Los Angeles Times about visiting his boyhood streets for the first time in twenty years. 'As I walked slowly around the block and let the memories flood back,' he wrote, 'it seemed to me that my old neighborhood was a miracle—the greatest miracle that had ever visited the earth. Here, for the first time, people came from all the corners of Europe, the Near East and China — and lived side by side in close quarters and did not cut each other's throats.' There was something in the air, he believed, 'that made us feel maybe the other fellow's beliefs and background were all right too.'

However rosy Lewis's memories of his boyhood in Brownsville may have been, he left home early and quickly established what became a lifelong pattern of short stays and frequent moves. He quit high school at the age of sixteen, worked a variety of jobs with local newspapers, briefly attended both New York University and the College of the City of New York (finding 'neither institution suited him'), then spent the winter of 1929-1930 in Paris. He returned to America in March 1930, took a job as a sports reporter in Newark, New Jersey, then moved nearly halfway across the world to Shanghai, China. He spent the next two years there working as a reporter for *The China Press* and *The Shanghai Evening Post.*

Living in China may have satisfied his appetite for travel at first. In early 1933, Lewis returned to New York, took a job with *The New York World Telegram,* switched to *The New York Journal American,* got married, and rented an apartment in Manhattan — one of the few times he kept the same address for longer than a year. His time in China provided the material for his first ventures into fiction, which were short but action-packed. 'Tibetan Image', for example, tells of fortune hunters forced to abandon a million dollars' worth of silver fox pelts in the Gobi Desert when they are attacked by a pack of man-eating dogs. It appeared in *Argosy* magazine in November 1935 and was followed by others full of stereotypes of enigmatic, slightly sinister Chinese. He also tried his hand at writing for the stage, collaborating with a former reporter, Louis Weitzenkorn, on 'Name Your Poison'. In the play, a group of petty crooks take out a life insurance policy on a homeless derelict and then attempt — unsuccessfully — to kill him through a series of 'accidents.' The show opened for a pre-Broadway run in late January 1936 and closed after six performances. The play needed 'repairs' was the only explanation offered by its producer, who let his option lapse a few months later.

Although Lewis claimed he was happy with his job at the *Journal American,* a certain discontent with comfortable situations seems to have been part of his nature. As he later told Newsweek magazine, the idea for his first novel, *Gentleman Overboard,* came to him as he stood on the roof on his apartment in Greenwich Village one evening in late 1936. Lewis looked down on the street below and considered what would happen if he fell: 'How would a man bridge that dizzy mental gap between the security under his feet and that world "down there"?' He decided to write a story to find out. To emphasize that mental gap, he chose as the subject of his experiment not an itinerant reporter like himself but a man whose very being embodies security.

Henry Preston Standish, the gentleman of *Gentleman Overboard,* is as solidly attached to the bedrock of the American establishment as a man could be. His family name evokes the English man of arms who sailed with the first Pilgrims on the Mayflower, the subject of 'The Courtship of Miles Standish', a Henry Wadsworth Longfellow poem memorized by generations of schoolchildren. Graduate of Yale, partner in a Wall Street investment bank, member of the Finance Club, Athletic Club and Weebonnick Golf Club, owner of a comfortable apartment on the Upper West Side, faithful husband and loving father of two, Standish is the epitome of a solid citizen. 'He drank moderately, smoked moderately, and made love moderately; in fact, Standish was one of the world's most boring men'. When Standish contemplates the prospect of a world without him, he thinks with regret that 'New York City would be dotted with spaces that could never be filled by anyone but the real Henry Preston Standish'.

And yet, like Lewis, Standish feels an irresistible urge to leave and find something that was missing at home.

In Standish's case, the impulse hits him out of nowhere. One day, sitting in his office, he 'suddenly found himself assailed by a vague unrest'. He feels compelled to get up, leave his office and take a walk along the Manhattan waterfront in Battery Park. As he looks out at the water, 'Forces beyond his control grasped him and shook him by the shoulders, whispering between clenched teeth: "You must go away from here; you must go away!"'

Standish does not understand this impulse. 'There was no sane reason why he must go away; everything was in its proper place in his life.' At the same time, his instincts tell him 'that he never would be able to breathe freely again unless he went far away.' Standish wasn't the first character in American literature to feel this urge to escape. Fifty years before *Gentleman Overboard,* Mark Twain's *Huckleberry Finn* lit out for the Indian Territory 'because Aunt Sally she's going to adopt me and sivilize me, and I can't stand it'. Perhaps what Lewis called 'security' was just another name for Huck Finn's 'sivilization'.

But when Standish sees the last sight of New York slip over the horizon as he sails away on a cruise through the Panama Canal to California, he feels as if 'all his weariness, all his doubts and fears, vanished magically into the sea'. In California, the sense of relief continues. Standish discovers 'a certain zest to things now that he had not experienced back home before; all his sensations were intensified'. He decides to keep going, to take another cruise, this time to Honolulu. 'Why, Henry?' his wife begs when Standish calls to break the news. 'I don't know', he replies. Even after he reaches Hawaii, he delays his return, exchanging his ticket back to San Francisco for a berth on the *Arabella,* a freighter taking a leisurely three-week voyage from Honolulu to Panama.

Lewis then sets his experiment in motion. Early one morning, while most on the ship are asleep and Panama still at least ten days away, Standish slips on a spot of grease while strolling on deck and falls overboard. Lewis has put his subject about as far away from the security of a comfortable life in New York City as one can get — two thousand miles from Panama, three thousand miles from Hawaii, along an infrequently-traveled route. Even here, though, conventions manage to reach out and control Standish. After he surfaces, when there is still a chance of his being heard by someone on the *Arabella,* he finds himself 'doomed by his breeding': 'The Standishes were not shouters; three generations of gentlemen had changed the trumpet in the early Standish larynx to a dulcet violoncello'. Standish hesitates to cry out and the *Arabella* steams away, its crew and other passengers oblivious to his plight. Another twelve hours pass before his absence is confirmed — and, in a cruel irony foreshadowing Lewis's own death, some onboard conclude that Standish's accident was, in fact, suicide.

With cool precision, Lewis peels back the layers of 'sivilization' as the hours pass and his subject tries to stay afloat, waiting to be rescued. Standish kicks off his shoes, then bit by bit removes his clothes, until he is naked, his eyes and lips scorched by the sun. At first, he feels embarrassed at making the *Arabella* turn around and rescue him; then pride in his 'tremendous adventure' of staying alive until his rescue; and finally, when he realizes there is no hope, of regret. 'And with each thought a pang came to his heart that had shattered, a pang of regret that he could not go on like other men having new extraordinary experiences day after day'. Extraordinary experiences like his heart 'having gone on beating thirty-five years without once stopping'; like never having gone hungry; like having been given everything he had ever desired. In the end, there is just one desire that will not be satisfied: to live.

When Lewis finished writing *Gentleman Overboard,* his own situation was precarious. He'd been living beyond his means, borrowing money and falling months behind in his rent. Just weeks before Viking published *Gentleman* in May 1937, Lewis declared bankruptcy with debts of $3,100 — over a year's income for a newspaperman — and no assets, except possible royalties from the book. It would not be the last time he found himself flat broke. Reviews of *Gentleman Overboard* began appearing soon after — the first on May 23 in *The New York Times,* the same paper in which his bankruptcy notice had appeared. Reviewer Charles Poore called the book 'entertaining' and 'a flight of fancy,' but sensed Lewis's underlying design: 'Standish seems to be undergoing an experiment rather than an experience'.

The book's brevity seems to have led many reviewers to consider it insubstantial. 'It is a good enough book of its kind, but it is one of those stories that might have been a masterpiece and is by no means one,' William Rose Benet wrote in *The Saturday Review.* Only Arnold Palmer, reviewing the British edition published by Victor Gollancz in the magazine *Britannia and Eve,* saw the book's length as a virtue: 'He has told, with unusual skill and intensity, a story which ninety-nine writers in a hundred would have ruined by expanding into a full-length novel or compressing to the requirements of a magazine editor'. Evelyn Waugh on the other hand, writing in *Time and Tide,* thought it wasn't short enough: 'In spite of its brevity it is too long; a Frenchman could have told the story in 50 pages.' Viking issued a second printing; Gollancz did not.

Hollywood came to Lewis's rescue. In August 1937, *The Hollywood Reporter* announced that Metro Goldwyn Mayer had signed Lewis as a 'term writer' — a staff writer with a contract for a term, usually six months, at the then-lucrative salary of $250 a week. Lewis, his wife Gita and their infant son Michael headed for California, arriving in early September 'in our original protoplasmic state', as he wrote his brother Ben (on MGM stationery). By Christmas, Lewis could report that he was busy working on a remake of the silent movie *Tell It to the Marines* and expected to 'be here for a long time'.

He was still struggling to pay off his debts, though. He wrote Ben that people were 'pressing me for debts and making my life miserable by threatening to sue me and attach my salary'. 'All the other writers live in big houses and entertain', he complained, 'and we live in a shack'. MGM shelved the remake of *Tell It to the Marines* and Lewis's contract was not extended. He was able to get a job with RKO, collaborating with Ian Hunter on *Fisherman's Wharf* and *Escape to Paradise,* a pair of B-movie musicals starring the boy tenor Bobby Breen, both released in 1939 and both formulaic and forgettable. By the end of that year, Lewis quit RKO and moved back to New York City with a job offer from the J. Walter Thompson advertisement agency and the manuscript of a second novel in hand.

Lewis's anti-war sentiments had been stirred by the outbreak of war in Europe. In *Spring Offensive,* Peter Winston, a young American out of work, unhappy in love and at odds with the isolationist mood in America, concludes 'There was no place for him in his own country' and travels to England to enlist in the British Army. When he completes his training and deploys to France as part of the British Expeditionary Force, however, he finds there is nothing to do in the months of stalemate known as the Phony War. He decides to make a small protest by sneaking into the no-man's land between the Maginot and Siegfried lines and planting a packet of sweet pea seeds. As Winston crouches there planting his seeds in the early hours one morning, however, the Phony War comes to an abrupt and violent end. He finds himself stranded between the two sides, unarmed and with little chance of survival. Like Standish in his last moments, Winston loses all hope: 'There was no one who wanted him anywhere'. A shell strikes and Winston is obliterated.

Lewis's timing could not have been worse. *Spring Offensive* was published in late April 1940. Two weeks later, German panzers began rolling into Belgium, France, and the Netherlands. By the end of June, France had capitulated. 'For its own sake, this slender novel should have made its appearance well before the beginning of the actual Spring Offensive', concluded *The Saturday Review.* Ralph Ellison predicted in his *New Masses* review, 'little will be said of it these days in the capitalist press'. He was right: the book sank without a trace.

Lewis still had hopes for his career as a novelist, though. Convinced that his handicap had been trying to write while holding down a full-time job, he took his family, now including a baby girl, Jane, to quiet Provincetown, Massachusetts. There he wrote his third novel. Focused on the residents of a rooming house in Greenwich Village on Christmas Eve, *Season's Greetings* is a love-hate letter to New York City. Lewis allowed himself a much richer prose style; the book is filled with vivid descriptions:

> Slowly the noises of the city came to life, autos shifting gears, horns honking, doors slamming shut, trains rumbling underground, machines chugging and whirling, feet tramping, babies wailing, children shouting, peddlers calling their wares. Slowly the smells of the city came to life, coffee brewing, bacon frying, garbage stewing, chemicals churling in cauldrons.

Despite the vitality of Lewis's writing, though, his subject once again was grim: 'the problem of loneliness in a city of eight million people'. One of the residents is a German refugee without a single friend or acquaintance in his new country. Another is an embittered alcoholic, a third an old woman who has outlived her family. Although some of the residents come together to create, for a few hours at least, a sort of community, Lewis refuses a happy ending for all. As his neighbours gather for an impromptu Christmas party, one resident, Mr. Kittredge, who began the day convinced 'there was no purpose in living any longer,' finds that nothing in the course of the day has changed his mind. He quietly slips out to Washington Park with a rifle and commits suicide — alone and unseen: 'Around the whole windswept park, in all the apartment houses and brownstone mansions and college buildings, not a single window opened and not a single person looked out'. Less than ten years later Lewis himself died alone and unseen in the Hotel

Earle — directly across the street from the park.

Published in September 1941, *Season's Greetings* received favourable but not glowing reviews. *The New York Times'* reviewer called it 'a story that pulses with feeling for the complex and comprehensive personality of New York'. *The American Mercury* did not care for Lewis's change of style: 'Overwritten in spots, it belabors its point, yet it holds the reader's interest'. Once again, Lewis was a victim of bad timing. After the Japanese attack on Pearl Harbor on December 7th, few Americans were in the mood to buy books about Christmas. The short biographical sketch on the back of *Season's Greetings* mentioned that the author and his family had returned to New York and promised that 'This time Mr. Lewis expects to stay home for good'. It didn't work out that way.

After working for *The New York Herald Tribune* as a reporter for about a year, Lewis tried again to make it on his own as a writer — without much luck. As *Los Angeles Times'* film industry reporter Fred Beck later told the story, by late 1942, Lewis 'was a small, sad man, shivering on the streets of New York'. A short story Lewis had written, 'Two-Faced Quilligan', had been rejected by 33 magazines and he worried that his family 'would have salami for Christmas dinner'. As Beck put it, 'Herbie wished somebody he knew would come along so he could borrow a buck'. Instead, Lewis came home to find an acceptance letter from *Story* magazine and a check for $50 — enough for a generous Christmas and a month or two more. Soon after, *Variety* reported that 20th Century Fox had bought the movie rights for the story and hired Lewis as a writer for $500 a week. Lewis and family returned to Los Angeles.

Despite the turnaround in his financial situation, Lewis was never content in Hollywood. 'Life is rather dull here', he wrote his brother Ben in July 1943. 'It's completely unreal going to the studio every day and writing scripts about make-believe people while the real people are cutting each other's throats with gusto everywhere'. In November he complained, 'I look around me and see the things that success buys out here, and I don't like any of them. Swimming pools get full of dead flies and uninvited guests. Big houses get full of live flies and uninvited guests'. Lewis wrote that he had decided to take a job offer with radio comedian Fred Allen and move the family back to New York. Fred Beck made the news public in *The Los Angeles Times* with a sly aside: 'Fred Allen has a new writer, brand new, and I'm just wondering if everybody is now going to be happy now that they've got what they wanted'.

The answer was no. Lewis expected to replace several writers who expected they were about to be drafted. They weren't. After eight weeks with Allen's show, Lewis decided 'I was tired of taking money under false pretenses' and returned to Hollywood. Lewis continued with 20th Century Fox, which released the movie version of Lewis's story, *Don Juan Quilligan,* in June 1945. As little as he cared for the work, Lewis desperately needed the studio's money. In early 1945, he complained to Ben that 'the Internal Revenue Bureau has attached my salary to make me pay off an old tax debt to Uncle Sam, which cuts down my fun, finances and practically eliminates (for the next few months) all the plans we had to send you our wedding gift'.

Lewis's only break from the studio grind came in May 1945 when he, Dalton Trumbo, and four other writers were sent on a six-week tour of combat areas in the Southwest Pacific at the invitation of General Henry 'Hap' Arnold, head of the U. S. Army Air Corps. 'I'm really seeing the war on this 16,000-mile junket,' he wrote from Guam on June 16, 1945: 'the planes, the fleet, the infantry, almost everything else'.

The war ended just two months after Lewis's return from the trip. He sold more stories: 'D-Day in Las Vegas' to RKO and 'The Fifth Avenue Story', which Lewis co-wrote with Frederick Stephani, to Liberty Films. Filmed as *It Happened on Fifth Avenue,* the story earned Academy Award nominations for the two writers in 1947. By then, though, Lewis's life had begun to fall apart. He was drinking heavily and taking barbiturates to help him sleep. His son Michael remembers seeing his father 'naked and completely comatose, in a chair' around this time. 'My mother told me it was alcohol and seconal'. Gita Lewis had begun to work for studios as a writer herself. As Michael recalls, 'my & my sister's real parents' during this time were the full-time maids his parents hired. The couple separated in July 1947.

Lewis's professional life was also coming apart. In January 1947, he became a member of the editorial staff of *The Screen Writer,* the magazine of the Screen Writers Guild. Unfortunately, the Guild was about to become the focus of Federal Bureau of Investigation inquiries into possible Communist infiltration of the motion picture industry. Working in support of the U. S. House Un-American Activities Committee , the F.B.I. interviewed dozens of witnesses and collected thousands of documents related to liberal political activities in Hollywood. An F. B. I. informant identified Lewis as a member of the American Communist Party.

Whether the allegation was true or not, Lewis had taken up with the losing side. Once again, his timing was terrible. He joined over 100 writers, actors, directors, and musicians signing a full-page advertisement protesting the House committee's hearings — which only added to suspicions about his politics. A month later, Dalton Trumbo and nine other members of the Screen Writers Guild were cited for contempt of Congress for refusing to testify before the committee. A group of the most powerful studio executives met in New York in December 1947 and issued a statement vowing, 'We will not knowingly employ a Communist or a member of any party or group which advocates the overthrow of the Government of the United States'. The practice of blacklisting had begun. 'The swimming pools are drying up all over Hollywood. I do not think I shall see them filled in my generation', Lewis remarked to a reporter, jokingly. But he did not take the experience so lightly. He suffered a nervous breakdown in mid-1948 and was unable to work for a year.

In September 1949, he returned to New York City for what would be the last time — alone. His wife Gita chose to stay in Hollywood. He took a job as rewrite man for *The New York Mirror.* 'I've enjoyed myself thoroughly and straightened myself out completely', he wrote Ben from New York in October 1949, adding that he'd sold several of his stories to provide an allowance for Gita and the children. Michael Lewis recalls that 'the four of us tried living together again as a family' in New York around Christmas 1949, but the marriage may have reached a breaking point. Gita took Michael and Jane back to Hollywood and moved in with Tanya Tuttle, wife of blacklisted director Frank Tuttle, who had gone to France in search of work.

In April 1950, Lewis filed for bankruptcy, citing over $26,000 in debts and unpaid income taxes. He moved into a room at the Hotel Earle in Greenwich Village. Although once considered among the best residential hotels in the city, in 1950, the Earle was, in the words of the poet Dylan Thomas, who stayed there around the same time as Lewis, 'a pigsty'. Lewis moved from the *Mirror to Time* magazine, but he was still broke. He apologized to Ben for not being able to help pay their father's bills from a prostate operation.

In late September, he left *Time* — whether voluntarily or not is unclear. Three weeks later, he was found dead in his hotel room. Although his death certificate stated the cause was heart attack, some of his acquaintances believed Lewis had committed suicide — which, Dalton Trumbo wrote his wife, was 'sad, but no more than to have been expected'. 'The only food on which a drowning man could subsist was the hope of being rescued', Lewis wrote in *Gentleman Overboard.* Perhaps he had lost hope of being rescued himself.

He left little to his widow beyond the prospect of future sales of his writing — of which there were few. In December 1950, one of his early stories, 'Surprise for the Boys', was adapted for the CBS television series *Danger.* A few years later, a producer bought the rights to Lewis's story 'The Bride Wore Pajamas', but the film was never made. Finally, in 1959, Gita, now remarried, sold his unfinished novel *The Silver Dark* to Pyramid Books, a paperback publisher. Despite a cover plug by novelist Budd Schulberg proclaiming it 'A genuinely original and compelling novel', the book was never reviewed and never reissued. Less than a handful of copies remain in libraries worldwide.

The Silver Dark might have marked the end of Lewis's story. His work was ignored in studies of American novels. His film credits alone kept his name alive in occasional reference books. His daughter Jane died in 1985 from complications related to diabetes; his brothers both died in the late 1990s and his widow Gita in 2001. Only Michael, with a handful of his father's letters and one lone page from his journal, remained to remember Lewis.

In the spring 2009, I came across a review of *Gentleman Overboard* while browsing through the archives of *Time* magazine. 'What would it feel like to fall off a ship in mid-Pacific?' the reviewer asked. 'With as much calm authority as though he had fallen overboard himself, Herbert Clyde Lewis tells just what it feels like'. I was on the lookout for long-forgotten books with unique qualities and *Gentleman Overboard* sounded like a perfect candidate. I located a copy, read it and posted a short enthusiastic review. Without having seen the *Newsweek* article describing Lewis's original idea, I referred to the book as an experiment:

> What matters is not whether it succeeds or fails but simply seeing what happens. Lewis puts his subject into the experiment and observes. This novel holds his notes. Few scientists could have recorded the results with such an elegant and light touch. It's been said that a true artist knows when to stop ... and does. By this criterion alone, Herbert Clyde Lewis proves himself a true artist with *Gentleman Overboard.*

A few months later, I received an email from Diego D'Onofrio, an editor with La Bestia Equilatera, a small Spanish-language publisher in Buenos Aires. 'I would like to ask you', he wrote, 'Which neglected book do you recommend me to publish?' Not familiar with La Bestia's audience, I was reluctant to offer many suggestions, but replied, 'If I had to pick one off the top of my head that is very accessible to a wide range of readers, I guess I'd pick *Gentleman Overboard* by Herbert Clyde Lewis. It should be relatively easy to translate and has a strong narrative line that should grab most readers very quickly'. Diego thanked me and said he'd order a copy.

Diego and his editor-in-chief Luis Chittaroni loved the book. In May 2010, they contracted for a translation and scheduled the book for publication. The Spanish title would be *El caballero que cayó al mar* (The Gentleman Who Fell into the Sea). The challenge of publishing a neglected book in another language is considerable, D'Onofrio later wrote. 'Because nobody knows the author, not least the book, which is also not known in his native language ... the only tool you have to sell the book is that it must be extraordinary in itself'.

By this standard, *El caballero que cayó al mar* performed exceptionally well. Its early reviews were consistently enthusiastic: 'Simple y magistral. Sólo eso. Sencillamente eso', Alejandro Frías proclaimed in *El Sol de Mendoza:* 'Simple and masterful. Only that. Simply that'. Another reviewer called it 'una perlita': a little pearl. The book continued to win critical acclaim as its readership spread beyond Argentina. One of Spain's leading critics, Ignacio Echevarría, praised the book in his monthly column for *El Cultural* and in 2019, a feature on CNN Chile recommended it: 'Con magistral sencillez, Herbert Clyde Lewis lleva el relato a una dimensión filosófica' ('With masterful simplicity, Herbert Clyde Lewis takes the story to a philosophical dimension'). D'Onofrio reports that *El caballero* 'is the book with the most unanimous praise from our entire publishing house, which now has more than 90 books'.

Even as the Spanish translation was underway, Luis Chittaroni began to share PDF copies of the original U.S. edition with acquaintances in the Argentinian literary community. The novelist Pablo Katchadjian in turn recommended the book to his friend Uriel Kon, an Argentina-born Jew living in Jerusalem and then starting up his own small press, Zikit Books. Looking for English-language novels that could be easily translated and published in Hebrew, Kon found the book matched his criteria perfectly: 'Clear, elegant prose; a compelling, existential story; a book you can sit down and read in a night'. He arranged for a Hebrew translation and Zikit published the book in June 2013.

The book struck a chord among Israeli readers. A feature review in *Ha'aretz,* one of Israel's most widely read newspapers, called it 'A miniature masterpiece that emerged from oblivion'. Zikit printed 1,00 copies — a number Kon considered 'somewhat optimistic' at the time. That edition sold out in under two months and Zikit went on to sell over 7,000 copies. 'There are around three to four thousand serious literary readers in Israel', Kon estimated. 'By that standard, this was a huge best-seller — a cult classic'. Standish's predicament — lost and forgotten in a great ocean — Kon believes, 'Resonated with many Israeli intellectuals who felt themselves isolated—not only as Jews surrounded by the Arab world but also unheard in a society dominated by conservative forces'.

In September 2020, Auteursdomein, a small press based in Amsterdam, published a Dutch translation: *Overboord.* This edition was sponsored by Dutch novelist Pauline van de Ven, who had come across *Gentleman* in a box of old books and ashtrays left by a distant uncle. As she wrote, 'I read it without interruption from cover to cover and was impressed by the austere language, the strong images and the universal scope of the haunting story'. For van de Ven, the book's power lies in its appeal to a paradoxical sense of 'shared loneliness'. It belongs, she believes, in 'same gallery of honor' as Leo Tolstoy's *The Death of Ivan Ilyich,* another short novel about a prosperous businessman facing his imminent death: 'It's an existentialist masterpiece'.

And now, Boiler House Press brings Herbert Clyde Lewis's 'little pearl' back to English readers, inaugurating Recovered Books, its new series aimed at restoring the work of long-neglected writers for today's audience. The rescue of *Gentleman Overboard* reminds us of the need to search, constantly, for the words of those writers who – through hardships, bad timing, or sheer accident – have fallen from literary history and become forgotten. If we take care to listen, we will find they still have things to tell us.

> Still looking for lost people – look unrelentingly.
> 'They died' is not an utterance in the syntax of life
> where they belonged, no *belong* – reanimate them
> not minding if the still living turn away, casually.
> ...
> The souls of the dead are the spirit of language:
> you hear them alight inside that spoken thought.
>
> From 'Listening for lost people' by Denise Riley
> from *Say Something Back* (London: Picador, 2016)

Gentleman Overboard
By Herbert Clyde Lewis

First published in this edition by Boiler House Press, 2021
Part of UEA Publishing Project

Cover Design and Typesetting by Louise Aspinall
Typeset in Arnhem Pro
Printed by Tallinn Book Printers
Distributed by NBN International

ISBN: 978-1-913861-23-0